THE CRAZY WORLD OF

OPHELIA RAMSBOTTOM

(120 DAYS OF HER LIFE)

Robin Anderton

Introduction

Good morning. Well by way of an introduction my name is Ophelia Ramsbottom a cross I have had to bear the last 48 years I have been on the planet, for the first 23 years my maiden name was Weeklea which was no better!

I live alone, sadly two years ago my husband of forty-six years has moved on to pastures new. He hasn't died, he has just moved in with the cow that dwells in the pastures new, who has the name of Heather. A 52 year old blonde Yoga instructor.

I live in a little village just outside the town of Snobihill called Little Hampton on the Rise. A name which seems to amuse ardent Goon fans, who regularly visit the village to take selfies next to the village signpost.

My address had always been an enigma to me until I investigated the Village history. In 1937 Rudyard Kipling died and as the village had had two new cul-de-sacs built in the same year, someone though it would be a good idea to name them "Ruddy Close" to save money on the lettering and "Just So Close" after the great man himself and his work. I managed to secure number 2 Ruddy Close, an address which everyone finds amusing.

The Village has a Pub called the Corn and Callus, A small Grocery Store we all call the Two Stop shop as invariably the Villagers forget to get everything, they went for the first time due to the average age of the Village residents being well over sixty. It also has a

Church and a Village Hall which has a thriving social calendar and various clubs ranging from Art Classes to Zumba of which I am a member of many as you will see as the year progresses, assuming I survive to the end of it.

Wednesday 31st December

This diary really should include New Year's Eve. I thought I was in for a cosy night by the fire, when the doorbell rang at 11pm.

It was the Major who lives at number six Ruddy Close, the Major is a stout gentleman who sounds a bit like Winston Churchill but looks very much like Jimmy Edwards. His waistcoat buttons appeared to be straining to remain in touch with the cloth, I feared that they may well shoot off any moment and take out my eye. He has lived alone ever since I have lived here.

"Hello Old Gal" he said as I peered around the door, "Couldn't help noticing your light was on, I've got another enormous roman candle and wondered if you like to join me in lighting it's touch paper on the stroke of midnight."

The Major had bought a box of twenty large roman candles for the millennium, he had let one off every year since, the trouble is the Majors touch paper gets damper every year. Last year it was almost 12.45am before we got a spark, and then it was more of a fizz than a bang. I declined his offer, thinking to myself I would rather have a Stroke at midnight than look at the Majors roman candle.

I spent midnight thankfully on my own. Which is just as I like it, I did hear shouts of "light you bugger" from the Majors garden about 1.30am, before drifting off to sleep.

Thursday 1ˢᵗ January

Happy New year!

I did wonder what this year would have install for me, only to find the weather being grey and raining.

Furthermore, I had forgotten I had run out of milk and had only two slices of bread both of which had turned blue in colour over the Christmas period. I hope this isn't indicative of the year ahead.

Fortunately, we have a Grocery / Post Office in the village which opens every day except Christmas day, this being the one-day Angus Khan the owner could make a fortune just selling parsnips, stuffing and batteries!

I donned my coat and walked to the shop which is about two hundred yards from where I live.

Well you wouldn't believe the commotion going on as I walked into the shop, it was like a Celtic feud.

What with Mr Khan's strong Scottish accent and Bernadette O'Leary's strong Irish accent I thought the

Battle of Benburb had started up again!

Apparently, Bernadette had opened a tin of alphabet spaghetti for her son to eat on Christmas day. "The holiest of days" Bernadette proclaimed.

Listening to this I did wonder who eats tinned spaghetti on Christmas day?

Anyway, Bernadette was not happy as this particular tin had been purchased at Mr Khan's shop.

While the whole of Bernadette's entire Family (Of which there are many) enjoyed the traditional Christmas dinner, Dermot her five-year-old son insisted as he does every day on his favourite tin of alphabet spaghetti.

The dinner was ready, the turkey carved, everyone sitting around the table ready when Bernadette bought in Dermot's alphabet spaghetti on toast.

Unfortunately, this particular tin only had four different letters in it, not the four letters Bernadette wanted to see!

"Christmas day" said Bernadette "Jesus's birthday and my son is looking down at his spaghetti and these awful four-letter words are staring back at him in every direction possible, all over his plate"

"Imagine my embarrassment" she went on "when my four sons and the rest of the family spotted the plate!

My eldest son Joseph asked if I had taken the other twenty-two letters out! I then had to spend thirty minutes picking out all the K's with a toothpick in order for

Dermot to eat anything"

Mr Khan proclaimed it was not his issue, as he didn't know what was in the tin.

But Bernadette wanted her money back and compensation for the shock.

Mr Khan then didn't help matters by offering a twenty five percent refund for the K.s taken out and offered her eighteen pence from the till.

Mrs O'Leary went mad and threw a carrot at Mr Khan who then phoned 999, Shouting "Help I am being assaulted by carrots, a bunch of them are attacking me" With his strong accent the lady at the emergency services misheard him and thought he had said clerics not carrots, the whole thing got very confusing.

I did try to calm things down. But with vegetables flying past my head, I decided to retire from the battle and left the shop. As Herman's Hermits use to sing "No Milk Today"!

What a start to the year.

Friday 2nd January

The sky is a lighter grey this morning so perhaps today will be a brighter start to the year.

I thought I would put the days weather down each day as it always feels like it is raining, I am sure it isn't!

I did venture to Mr Khan's Two Stop Grocery store and fortunately Mrs O'Leary was nowhere in sight, the same also could be said for the carrots!

He did thank me for trying to intervene yesterday and offered me a free tin of alphabet spaghetti as a gesture of goodwill. The tins themselves now had a notice above them stating "This shop is not responsible for any offensive words that may be contained is these tins"

"I see you have almost sold out" I said pointing at the last two tins, "Yes "said Mr Khan "There has been a rush for them since I put the sign up!"

I thanked him but declined his offer of a free tin and left with just the bread and milk.

This afternoon the Little Hampton on the Rise Knitting Circle, met for our fortnightly meeting.

Each year we have a theme throughout the year to help one charity or another, today it was as much about idea's as knitting. Jane Roid is the lady that runs the club which is attended by seven ladies and the rotund Mr Tway. Why he comes every fortnight nobody knows, he can't even knit.

He arrives with his French knitting dolly and corks away at quite a pace, producing miles and miles of a half inch snake. He never does anything with it, and hardly says a word.

I did once ask him what he intended to do with his snake, he just went red and looked at the floor!

His Christian name is Justin so I call him Justin the way, but he never takes the hint.

Anyway, ideas for this year were in abundance! Mrs Catterack aged 92, suggested balaclavas for the SAS. It was noted that these may get into the wrong hands and nobody in the club wanted to see their balaclava being used by a bank robber or an international terrorist. Jane Roid said she only had rainbow colours in her wool bag, so unless there was an incident at a Gay Pride Festival which required the services of the SAS, she wouldn't be able to help.

So as not to upset Mrs Catterack we told her that we would give it some thought.

Mrs Beaverbrook 88 years of age, shouted out "egg cosies" we could knit loads of those.

Everyone looked at each other not knowing how to react. "We could knit prime ministers through the ages, I can do Neil Kinnock, I like him" She continued "and that Robin Day"

I was about to inform her that neither Neil or Robin were prime ministers, when I noticed Jane Roid shaking her head.

"Good Idea Mrs Beaverbrook, but I thought we could do daffodils for Marie Curie again, it went very well last year" said Jane Roid. So it was agreed after a vote, 6 For 1 Against with Mr Tway abstaining as he didn't like getting confrontational where politics are concerned?

After such an intense debate, we had a cup of tea and our usual box of Black Magic Chocolates, something we indulge in and completely agree on each meeting. We then called it a day and arranged to meet again in two weeks' time. This week it was more natter than knitting.

Saturday 3ʳᵈ January

Very frosty this morning, and remained so for most of the morning,

This morning I am attending the Jan Gough Art Club at the Village Hall, it is a life class this morning and I was intrigued to know who the model was going to be. We have never done this before, but it was something to tick off my bucket list

As I left, the Major was just leaving his house too.

"Morning Ramsbottom" he said in a loud voice. "Off to the art class, are you? Me too" he said without waiting for my reply.

I suspected he would be attending if there was life class, just in case it was a young lady posing!

On arrival, the clubs ten ladies and one man sat behind our easels waiting in anticipation for the model to arrive. When to our surprise the Major appeared in a dressing gown. I say dressing gown it was made of red silk with a dragon on the back. He looked like Big Daddy entering the ring in drag, but with a slightly larger waistline.

"Morning artists" he said and gave me a wink as he dropped his robe to the floor. He then said "How do you want me?"

"With your clothes back on!" someone shouted

I almost wretched at the sight

The Major continued "Fortunately Ladies the cold weather hasn't penetrated my woollen britches so there's plenty for you to get on with!"

Miss Radish who thought it was a still life lesson, fainted and needed first aid.

Mrs Johnston asked for a larger sheet of paper and a bigger easel!

Bernadette O'Leary made the sign of the cross said a Hail Mary and hurriedly left the building clutching her rosary beads.

Mr Pickle the only male in the group, said "He didn't think he had enough lead in his pencil". To which Mrs Johnston replied "Unlike the Major" It was funny.

The Major stood there on a podium posing like Michelangelo's David albeit before Michelangelo had started chiselling.

Mrs Hargreaves and I had a rear view. It was like looking at the Grand Canyon, particularly when the Major bent over to move the dressing gown away. "There's somewhere to park your bike" I said. To which Mrs Hargreaves replied "There's enough room there for the front wheel of a penny-farthing!"

Mrs Johnston whispered under the breath "That reminds me I have some ironing to do when I get in!" and chuckled to herself.

After a lot of complaining the Major was asked to leave making an exit via the back door, he was replaced with a bowl of fruit and vegetables.

Although the placement of two aubergines and banana made it difficult to erase the memory of what we had been subjected to earlier.

At this point Miss Radish came round still bleary eyed, took one look at the bowl and fainted again.

Mrs Catterack with her poor eye sight didn't even realise the Major had left!

Yet her painting was still an accurate representation and won the best painting of the day.

Mrs Beaverbrook surprisingly didn't complain at all, we then realised she was asleep.

I need younger friends!

Sunday 4ᵗʰ January

Frosty again, just like I will be to the Major when I see him.

National Obesity Week. Like I need reminding!

Exciting times a new Waitloads supermarket opens today in Snobihill.

My friend of twenty years Mrs Emily Ponkhurst. No, her name isn't mis-spelt, although the similarities are there and not only in name. About fifteen years ago there was a rumour that the local swimming pool was going to close. Emily immediately started her campaign called "Vote for Swimming". She even chained herself to the railing of the top diving board at the baths she was trying to save. Three hours she was up there, to be honest it was an hour before anyone noticed her. Emily embarrassingly shouting "Vote for swimming" in a swimming pool, everyone thought she was the local crackpot and took no notice. Then there was the time she fell in front of a horse and almost died. Well I say horse it was a clothes horse on which she had been drying a very heavy damp John Lewis Egyptian cotton towel which then fell on top of her after she had tripped on a stickle brick, she very nearly suffocated under weight of the towel. It was her cocker spaniel Joe who saved the day by pulling it off her. She was saved by the skin of his teeth.

That aside my morning began after breakfast with Emily picking me up in her smart car at as we are going shopping in Snobihill this morning. The car is far too small for her as she is a large lady with a rather large bosom. She tooted her horn on arrival and I duly left the house and squeezed into the limited available space on the passenger side. I wasn't sure whether the car was being guided by her hands or breasts as both seemed to be in contact with the steering wheel. Thankfully it is an automatic gear box as finding the gear stick would have been a lost cause.

I then noticed that each time she braked the horn tooted due to the unavoidable contact between her breasts and steering wheel.

This in turn aggravated all the drivers on the way, who appeared to be impersonating Ted Rogers 321 finger gesture but without the three! They did look angry.

Thankfully we arrived in one piece, Emily parked in a Parent Child space, leaving a teddy bear on the seat. "Works every time" she said and smiled.

Emily said she needed new underwear and naturally I thought we were heading for M&S, when to my horror she took a left straight into Ann Summers. "It's a good fit here" she said seemingly unaware of the articles on the walls all around. She then picked up a bra with tassels. Emily noticed the look of surprise on my face. "Don't worry, I use the tassels on my cushions" she said. Thankfully we were done in ten minutes, the longest ten minutes of my life.

On leaving, unfortunately I bumped straight into Jane

Roid "You won't find any wool there!" she shouted followed by a loud laugh. Jane Roid then disappeared before I could say anything. How embarrassing.

We then headed for the new very upmarket Waitloads. It was very nice. I bought two items and went to pay at the self-checkout.

I put my plastic shopping bag in the bagging area, I tried to scan my first item and then heard "Surprising item in bagging area" from the machine. I tried again only to hear "Surprising item in bagging area" The queue was now building. The lady behind me then then shouted loudly in a very posh accent "It's probably your Aldi bag, we don't get many of those in here" she then turned to her husband for approval, he smiled back at her "Very good Dear" he said, to which I addressed him and totally ignored her."I see you have bought your Bag for Life with you, what's her name?" I said, pointing to the wife, "I say, watch your lip" he said going almost a red as the cravat he was wearing. I then noticed the fresh Scandinavian Trout in his basket. "I see your replacing your old trout with a new one, good swap if you ask me" I said looking at his wife and then the Trout in the basket.

The rest of the customers found this very amusing. The manager came over at this point and asked Emily and I to leave. He then apologised to the posh lady for any inconvenience calling her by name Mrs Pengleton-Smithe or something. I then turned to the Manager "And your plums aren't as firm as they should be" I said, to further laughter from the queue.

Emily dragged me away before I could say anymore.

I was livid. "Woe betide anyone who sticks a finger or two up at your horn on the way home" I said.

We then burst into laughter and headed home. OAP rebels without a cause!

I was glad to get back to Little Hampton.

Never a dull moment!

Monday 5th January

Driving rain and cold this morning.

I have stopped in today as the weather is so awful. I decided to clean my kitchen cupboards out and spruce them up this morning. To my amazement I found a packet of Spangles, a silver threepence and a programme from 1956 FA Cup Final between Manchester City and Birmingham City.

I couldn't understand how I hadn't spotted them before. To be honest I was tempted by the Spangles after all there wasn't a "Best before date" but the 4d price label did put me off.

After cleaning the cupboards, I put a sticky note inside the cupboard with "Last cleaned 5th Jan" written on it, to remind me.

Although I suspect that it will never be done again, it's

too much like hard work.

It was a University of the Third Age (U3A) meeting this afternoon, each month we have a guest speaker.

I met Miss Blinkensop on her way to the Village Hall, she was dragging behind her an enormous trunk, which I had to help her with. Miss Blinkensop is a tiny lady who is always dressed from head to toe in tweed, she is 75 years old, never married and still looking for Mr Right, although these days I think she should settle for Mr Not Quite Right, it would be a perfect match!

She has always said when talking about men that she had had far too many taster sessions but never a main course and certainly not dessert!

This afternoon Miss Blinkensop was very excited, as she explained this is the day she shared her interest in thimbles with the U3A members at the Village Hall. She was thrilled I had taken the time to come and listen to her lecture. I had forgotten about this and was only going to check on the date on the Village Hall notice board for the speed dating evening I had seen advertised. Already I was regretting leaving the house! I now felt obliged to stay.

Twenty people were at the meeting, on seeing Miss Blinkensop and the size of the trunk, four members immediately made an excuse and left. Another member said with dismay "Are you sure that talk is today?"

Miss Blinkensop was soon up on the stage, trunk open and getting box after box of thimbles from the enormous case, there must have been at least two hundred.

Then promptly at 2pm Miss Blinkensop held thimble number one high in the air and commenced her talk entitled "Thimbles, my life at the tips of my fingers"

She began by telling us where she had purchased the thimble, including a description of the shop and its owner. How much the thimble had cost, the year it was purchased and why she had purchased it. She also said "Could you save any questions until the end?" What could anyone possibly ask?!

An hour and a half had past listening to Miss Blinkensop and we were only on the description of thimble number sixty-three, the one she had won at the fair on the "Hook a duck" stall while on holiday in Ramsgate in 1961. The stall owner being slim build with a moustache?

I think Mr Roid who had been fidgeting in his seat for the past hour repeated the words "hook a duck" under his breath at least it sounded like "hook a duck"!

Fortunately, at this point Mrs Rogers Head of the U3A action committee fainted.

I have never seen so many people rush to someone's aid in all my life.

Miss Blinkensop held aloft thimble sixty-four the special one from Windermere, she paused waited a while and then sat down.

I knelt over Mrs Rogers feeling for a pulse, when she

opened one eye, winked and closed it again.

"Under the circumstances I think we will have to abandon your very interesting talk Miss Blinkensop" Mr Roid shouted across the room.

To my amazement three members were genuinely disappointed and asked if it could be continued some other time.

Once Miss Blinkensop had put most of her thimbles away, Mrs Rogers was sitting on a chair sipping a cup of water and looking very ashen considering the charade she was playing.

"Sometimes being head of the action committee, you have to take action for everybody's sake" Mrs Rogers whispered to me.

As we all left the hall, I checked the date for the speed dating and helped Miss Blinkensop home with her trunk.

Why does this always happen to me?

Tuesday 6th January

The sun shone for an hour this morning and then rained all day.

I received a letter in the post today from the Highways Agency, I won't go through the whole letter but the gist of it is, they want to put sleeping policemen on the main road through Little Hampton on the Rise.

A wide-awake Policeman would be a better option, as we haven't seen one of those in Little Hampton for years.

Not since 1997 when the elderly Mr Jackson (Now deceased) who lived at 8 Ruddy Close attacked the Majors Peony with his secateurs. It got very heated, the Major fetched his hoe from his garden shed to help fend Mr Jackson off who was like Edward Scissorhands on speed.

That all started because the Major couldn't keep his Peony under control and let it wander into Mrs Jacksons beautifully manicured bush. Mr Jackson complained week after week to the Major but to no avail. The final straw came when it encroached on her pink clematis. Mr Jackson lost the plot and lashed out with his secateurs.

A neighbour called the Police who arrived a half an hour later to sort it all out. By this time the Majors Peony was no more than a stump. It eventually went to court and Mr Jackson had an ASBO put on him, he was very embarrassed. The Major was told to keep his Peony under control in future. I don't think they ever spoke again. Mrs Jacksons Bush didn't get as much attention after that, it was never the same again and wilted as the years went by. Poor Mr Jackson died not long after the ordeal, some said it was the shame of it all, others said the electronic tag on his ankle had somehow caused his pacemaker to fail. Nothing was ever proven though and his death was put down as heart failure. On the plus side the Majors Peony made a full recovery and still blossoms today.

Anyway, the Sleeping Policemen are not required and I have now got a bee in my bonnet about the whole matter. Suddenly the year has a purpose.

I immediately phoned Emily who I was sure would take up the mantel with me. Of course, she agreed, I now had to rally my troops.

But not just at the moment as I was in the middle of baking a lemon drizzle for tomorrow's speed dating evening, I thought it might give me the edge over the competition. I am pretty sure that the recently widowed Mrs Tushingham would be there, and her cherry bakewell's are the talk of the Village.

I then phoned Gail of "Gail's Nails" the mobile beautician to come out and give my nails and face the once over ready for the speed dating tomorrow. Gail had moved to the area a couple of years ago from Dudley in the Black Country.

If you wanted any gossip you just booked Gail for a manicure and you get to know everything that's going on in the Village.

Unfortunately, it went to an answerphone message which her husband Wayne had done for her. I was greeted by his loud strong Black Country accent "Hi, if yam trying to get us yam out of luck cos we ain in. If yam hoping to have a Pedi, Mani, or fancy a Vajaz then leave your number and our Gail will get back to yer. Speak when yow hear the pip. Thanks Mate".

I winced and left my message. Hopefully she will ring

back.

Wednesday 7th January

Cold but the sun is shining.

I feel very upbeat this morning, Gail did ring back and
has booked me in for 12.43pm. She does state some odd
times, she never seems to round up or down like other
people. My last appointment was at 2.02pm!

This morning I decided to have a long soak in the bath as
this was a special day, it's not every day you may meet
the man of your dreams. I put a Gladioli and Fig bath
bomb in the bath water, which had been bought for me
last Christmas by Mrs Catterack from the Knit and
Natter Group.

It was fizzing foaming and bobbing around the bath like
a thing possessed, I slowly got in. I can't say it was a
pleasant experience. The damn thing disappeared and
went somewhere no-one has the right to go without
asking which caused me to jump and I burnt my toe on
the hot tap. Then it reappeared and got lodged between
my breasts and I couldn't shift it. My boobs were now
raising out of the water like a recently inflated life
jacket.

The scent of fig which had been promised now blasted
up my nostrils from very close range but was more like
the scent of fags than figs. It was awful, I eventually
dislodged the bomb and disposed of it. Not a good start
to the day. The low-cut blouse I was going to wear this
evening was certainly out of the question as I now had a

red rash in my cleavage. I had also taken on an aroma of a tobacconists.

Gail arrived at 12.46pm and apologised for being late!

She said that she had just come from Mrs Tushingham's and her Vajazzle had been a bigger job than expected!

I didn't dare ask why, but I was concerned that she was going to be better prepared for the speed dating than I could ever be, especially that I now had the rash. I settled for my usual nails and eyebrows and had some hide and heal applied to my cleavage. Unfortunately, Gail got so carried away telling me the local gossip that she inadvertently took most of my right eyebrow off. "Don't worry" she said "I can pencil it back in". Not what I wanted to hear. Gail left an hour later, leaving me with a perpetual look of surprise!

Later in the afternoon I assume I had an allergic reaction to the Hide and Heal as the rash now worsened and had travelled to my neck. I pulled a bright yellow polo cotton top from the wardrobe as this was the only thing with a high enough neck to cover the rash. It had been so long since I had worn this it smelt of bread and butter, it was also a size 12, I am now a size 16. This was the only thing available as time was now short. I sprayed it with Lemongrass Frabreze stretched and ironed it, leaving it by the open window to air.

Things were not going to plan.

To top it all my curling tongs then overheated and singed my fringe. I looked ridiculous.

I arrived at the Village Hall clutching my lemon drizzle not feeling very confident, I pushed open the inner hall doors and was immediately struck by a dazzling light, at first, I thought it was the Glitterball catching the light but then realised it wasn't from the ceiling but much lower. Mrs Tushingham sat right opposite the door, sitting like she was Sharon Stone waiting to be interviewed by Michael Douglas, with her Vajazzle catching the light each time she crossed her legs.

I ignored her completely and headed for Emily who was waving at me. "What's happened to you?" she said. "Don't ask" I replied.

The room now had about ten ladies sitting behind the tables that were placed individually around the edge of the room. I was quite pleased as there wasn't a great deal of competition. Mrs Bingham must be ninety, Mrs Windbarg has a dodgy hip and Miss Everton is hard of hearing. The one lady who I didn't recognise had bought her knitting so no worries there. Mrs Tushingham though looked very confident crossing her legs more times than Kenny Everet, and it wasn't in the best possible taste!

Jane Roid explained the format for the evening, stating that we would spend four minutes with each gentleman and rotate when she rang the bell.

She then continued "I am sorry to say at present we only have four gentlemen present so please be patient".

The men then emerged from the side room. Before I had

even had chance to see who they were or what they looked like. The lady next to me said "Not for me" stood up and walked out.

I then realised why. The Major, Mr Tway, Mr Ditherington who donned a patch over one eye and finally Father Aweigh!? who explained he had been asked just to make the numbers up. The four stood before us.

"Gentlemen please start on the right and work your way around the room" shouted Jane Roid and then rang her bell.

The Major made a bee line for my table. "By God Gal, I thought it was a "Murder Mystery" night with Colonel Mustard" he exclaimed nodding at my yellow top, "If you're looking for the lead piping then look no further" he said with a suggestive wink and a smile. I knew then, this was going to be a very long four minutes!

Never has a bell sounded so sweet to my ears, but even before I could let out a sigh of relief Mr Tway was sitting opposite me, he looked at the floor for four minutes not saying a word.

Then Mr Ditherington had such a strong west country accent I thought I was being interviewed by Captain Hook or should that be Doctor Hook. Anyway, I could hardly understand a word he said.

Finally, Father Aweigh sat down and asked why I hadn't been to church lately. What a great night!

I was please to get a cup of tea and a slice of cake, while the rest of the Ladies suffered as I had.

We then had to fill out a score card for each candidate. Surprisingly I didn't rate any of the men above three out a ten.

We had all finished and Jane Roid was about to read out the scores when the door opened a man entered aged about 40 years. "Tall dark and handsome" Emily whispered to me.

I have never seen so many ladies dash back to their seats so quickly in all my life. I made sure I was on table one. Jane Roid approached the man "Well better late than never all the ladies are waiting to grill you one by one" she said with a smile and directed him to my table.

My opening gambit was "Do you like older women" straight to the point I thought. "Yes" he replied

"I pick up older ladies all the time" he went on. "Really" I said thinking him rather forward.

My second question was "Would you be averse to taking me out?" "Not at all, I'll take you out anytime, just call me" he replied.

This was going so well. I thought I would throw my curve ball question at him.

"Would you ignore a no entry sign and carry on up the avenue" I said raising the one eyebrow I had left.

"Not with the old banger I'm riding at the moment, it's

too risky" he replied with a smile.

"So coarse" I thought "Would you be available Friday" I said boldly.

"I think so. What time?" He said.

My heart was now pounding at last I thought a date is on the cards.

Jane Roid then rang the bell. "Move on to table two please" she said.

Mrs Bingham then interrupted "Is this going to take long as I need to be home by 8.30pm?"

"I don't think so Mrs Bingham do you want a lift home?" enquired Jane Roid "No, I already have one this young man is my Ring and Ride driver!"

The evening was then closed with an air of disappointment, The Major had given everyone a ten, Mrs Tushingham had given the Major a six, his highest score of the night making them a match!

Father Aweigh had two matches, which I found weird. He refrained from taking them up.

I arrived home at 8.48pm. Before going to bed I had a glass of the Japanese Brandy I had won at the Christmas Bazaar. The bottle I vowed I would never touch, but this had been a dramatic day.

Thursday 8ᵗʰ January

Weather Glum and Gloomy

As is my head, I have no idea what was in that Brandy but I woke up this morning on the bathroom floor. I have no recollection as to how I got there, my bed was still made and has not been slept in.

The slightest noise hit my eardrums like a thunderbolt sending a pain through my head. The clock struck 11am, if that wasn't loud enough the telephone rang. I answered it just to stop the infernal ringing in my ears. "Little Hampton 5736" I announced in a whisper holding the phone to my ear. Unfortunately, it was Miss Everton, the lady who is hard of hearing that I had been making conversation with last night. "HELLO" she shouted. "ARE YOU THERE" she continued. "YES" I shouted down the phone. My head was now pounding, apparently, I had agreed to take Miss Everton and her Parrot to the Vet this afternoon. She thinks "John" (The parrot was named after the snooker player) has asthma as he is very wheezy when he speaks.

My heart sank when I found myself shouting "I WILL PICK YOU UP AT 2PM". It was now 11.45am and I realised I had been shouting for fortyfive minutes. My throat was now sore and my ears where ringing.

I had a spot of lunch and ventured to Miss Everton's who lived in a cottage by a stream at the bottom of the Village. She was waiting by the door with the parrot in his cage. I tooted my horn and waved. "I'm coming, I'm coming" came a wheezy squawk. I wasn't sure whether it was Miss Everton or the Parrot speaking. Miss Everton got in with the cage on her lap thankfully she had put new batteries in her hearing aids. The Parrot just stared at me. "Your enormous" squawked the breathless Parrot. "Ignore him" said Miss Everton "he says that all the time" The Parrot then produced a sound which I can only associate with a steam train slowly leaving New Street station, this went on for five minutes. Very strange. We eventually arrived at the Vets, my ears still ringing and my headache was no better.

We were greeted by a very tall man in a green outfit, "Miss Everton" he enquired. "You're a big boy" said the Parrot. It was uncanny how he made some logic of the circumstances he was in. "I'm Mr Hollybush the Vet please follow me". "I'm coming, I'm coming" came another wheezy squawk. Once in the surgery the Parrot never shut up. Then he squawked "Stroke the Anaconda". Mrs Everton explained that she had bought him for £5 from a Pet Shop that was in the process of being closed down "I presume it had snakes" she said. The Vet got out his stethoscope. "I will just listen to his chest" said the Vet, the bird replied "What a magnificent chest" the Vet ignored this. Fortunately, the Parrot then went into his five-minute routine of the steam train impersonation again, so the Vet listened intently. Finally, there was a loud squawk and a cry of "Cover me in Marmite!". "He has never said that before" said Miss Everton surprised.

Mr Hollybush said it wasn't asthma and the parrot was

fine. "Just out of interest what pet shop did you buy him from" asked the Vet.

Miss Everton then explained "He was advertised for sale in the local newspaper, I went there with my neighbour to collect him, the pet shop was in the back streets of Birmingham. I think it was called "Pussies Galore" if I recall which was strange as there wasn't a cat in sight. The Lady who owned the place said the police had shut the place down the Parrot was the last bird left." I have no idea why the Police would close a pet shop. I paid £5 and left with the Parrot and cage.

Mr Hollybush looked at me with a smile and I quickly thanked him for his time and left very embarrassed.

Miss Everton is still none the wiser!

Friday 9th January

Weather Windy and Wet

Emily Ponkhurst visited me this morning, no idea why I put her full name as I only know one Emily, I knew she had arrived because her hoot tooted when she stopped outside my house!

Emily had arrived today to discuss what should be done about the Little Hampton High Street being humped. We haven't even got a school in the village, so I have no idea why it would be a Council priority.

Emily said that "Mrs Tushingham's cat had had a lucky escape a couple of months ago when Bob the Baker had run over the cat's tail in his van just outside the Two Stop shop". The Vet had to amputate the cat's tail, but Emily said that "she didn't think that would be the reason as Mrs Tushingham was quite happy with the outcome as now everyone thought the cat was a Manx and they are very expensive to buy!" "She doesn't recall her complaining to the Council but you never know"

We both knew that Mrs Tushingham was very much in favour of humping, and would probably head the campaign for those in support.

I think I need another reason to call Gail again as I needed the latest village gossip to gauge opinions.

"Ever thought about having a Vajazzle" I asked Emily. "Not a chance" she replied "I can't even be bothered to replace the mosaic tiles in the bathroom let alone that.

I booked the Village Hall for the 23ˢᵗ January for a meeting regarding the humping. I now had to come up with a poster and something catchy to put on it.

Then Emily shouted "Put this prevention into detention".

"I like it" I said, so that is what is on the poster and the time and date of course.

I then telephoned all the people I knew that I thought would be against this silly idea of humping.

Emily stayed for tea and our regular game of scrabble, but the board seemed to take on a life of its own. I'm not sure if it was because we were both angry, but some of the words were quite choice, the board ended up reading like a Quentin Tarantino script. My final word being Flagitium" extending Emily's "Flag"" and ending on a triple to win the game. This was disputed by Emily who immediately put on her coat and left shouting "Decipiat" (The Latin word for Cheat) to make a point, as she slammed the front door. She will be alright in the morning, she just doesn't like losing. I quickly poured the letters into the bag, before I had chance to reflect on what was put down. I was worried I would have nightmares.

I then made myself my special milky drink before going to bed. Three parts Horlicks and two parts Ovaltine. It's wonderful. I call it Horovalicks. It's a lot safer than japanese brandy! I just need to remember not to ask for it when I'm out, asking for Horovalicks may get me more than I bargained for!

Saturday 10th January

Snow flurries followed by rain

Not a day for going out Jane Roid phoned this morning to see how the knitted daffodils were coming along, I had to lie and say splendidly. I haven't made one!

I only had red wool so decided to go for poppy's instead, I sure no-one would mind. The trouble is my mind is now concentrating on the village speed bumps.

I received a rather battered parcel this morning but have no idea who sent it to me. The card inside read "Happy Christmas and have a wonderful 2008. Love as always T xxxx. "Surely it can't have taken over a decade to be delivered. I checked the date posted and sure enough it said Dec 2007!

I couldn't think who T was, or think of any Ts I knew in 2008. I opened the parcel hoping for a clue.

It contained a 2008 Diary, a luxury hot chocolate packet expiry date March 2010, and two tickets for Crippen the Musical for April 2008.

I then notice a note, which read "I Couldn't have done it without you. Just a little something to say thank you. T xx"

Unfortunately, the postmark was smudged so I couldn't tell where in the country it had been sent from. I don't know anyone beginning with the letter T.

This was going to drive me mad, I phoned Emily, she

had a list of T's "Tony the Plumber, Tarquin the Sword Swallower, Tupperware Trevor, Taxidermist Tom" she said. "But none of these would send me a parcel, and why are you assuming it's a man" I enquired. Emily then said "I bet it's Theresa's mother Theresa. Didn't you help her to lose weight in 2007. You remember her, I remember you saying that you would never have thought that you would be helping Mother Theresa as we use to call her, to lose weight. You remember?" But the fact is I didn't remember.

I put the phone down after exhausting every T I ever knew, and none the wiser.

This has driven me mad all day, the only person I could possibly think of was Titan my brother, but he said it wasn't him and anyway he calls himself Peter and has for years. Well it wasn't the best name to be given when your surname is Weeklea. I can't believe my parents didn't think or perhaps they did and had a cruel sense of humour. Ophelia and Titan Weeklea. Thanks Dad!

Mind you P Weeklea isn't much better!

Still none the wiser by bedtime, great day this has been.

Sunday 11ᵗʰ January

Gail force winds and heavy rain

I was thinking of going to Church this morning, but due to the constant tossing and turning all night thinking about the parcel, and then having a nightmare involving Mr T from the A team who burst out of a cardboard box shouting "Which Mother…….. wants a Hot Chocolate" which I won't write down, but it woke me up in a sweat at 3am. It took me ages get back off to sleep.

It was about 11.15am when I stirred, which is a shame as I was hoping to drum up some support at Church for the no humping campaign.

By the afternoon I was onto my tenth knitted Poppy, when the doorbell rang.

It was Father Aweigh. He said he was going door to door visiting his frail elderly parishioners to see if they wanted to be put on the Holy Communion at home list.

I was a bit taken aback at this, being classed as elderly was a bit of a shock too. But before I could say no, he was in my living room and my dining room table was set up like an altar with Father Aweigh kneeling in front of it, already reciting his second Hail Mary. I felt obliged to kneel next to him what else could I do? He then had that Incestuous (Not sure that's spelt right) smoke thing they wave about filling my living room with a smog. I did wonder if he was committing an exorcism at the same time, hopefully he could banish Mr T and I can get a good night's sleep!

Before the haze had cleared, I had taken both the body and the blood of Christ, and Father Aweigh was on his second cup of tea and had got through half of my packet of chocolate hobnobs.

I did manage though to get his point of view though on the humping in the Village, although he had gone very red before I explained I was talking about Sleeping Policemen.

Good news, he is on our side, if only for the sake of the suspension on his 1964 Morris Minor which gets far more of his attention than any of his flock.

Later it was Antiques Roadshow, bath without any bath bombs and an early night.

Monday 12th January

Raining

Not a day for going out, so I decided to give Lottie Thatcher a call. I had met Lottie when I worked part time at the local library many years ago. You have never seen a library so well run, Lottie knew where every book was, how many times it had been out and when it was due to be dusted! She could have taught Mr Dewey a thing or two, about his Decimal Classification System in the Library.

Lottie is now the Head of Stationery at the local council office. But most importantly she frequents with the top councillors so gets to know everything, this could be useful as I need to know what is going on with the village humping process. She is the most meticulous lady I know. Her attire is pretty much the same you could cut yourself on her trouser creases, and there is not a hair out of place in her bun.

I called her work number, the phone rang and then went straight to an answer phone message. "Ms Thatcher is unavailable please ring again using extension 3387".

This was strange as Lottie had never been late in her life, never mind having a day off.

I looked through my phone book and fortunately I had her home number.

The phone rang and then a very croaky voice answered, for a moment I thought I had called Miss Everton by mistake and that damn parrot had answered the phone. "Hello is that you Lottie?" I enquired.

"Is that you Ophelia?" came back the reply. Lottie then burst into tears. This was not the Lottie I know!

Lottie finally composed herself and explained the reason for her dismay.

As I said Lottie is head of stationery at the council, every pencil, pen and paperclip are accounted for and allocation of each item is recorded with precision. Woe betide anyone who uses their rubber to quickly and requests a new one. "That wreaks of inefficiency on every level" she once said.

The Council though over the past years have been making cutbacks, staff, pensions, salaries and of course stationery have all been victims to the cuts.

Lottie was up to the task and reduced her allocation of staff, her ink flow charts being the talk of the Council.

There was though a great deal of animosity amongst the staff, particularly regarding the salaries and pensions.

Anyway, when Lottie arrived back from lunch at 12.56pm on 4th January, there was a right kerfuffle in the office.

Someone had written "Save our Pens" in human excrement on the Ladies toilet wall.

There was an immediate enquiry, and Lottie was the main suspect being the head of stationery and so fastidious. Who else would be so passionate about pens?

"I've been suspended, subject to an enquiry" Lottie sobbed. "How could they think I could do such a thing?" she continued after taking a breath "It couldn't be me, do they not realised I would never end a sentence without a full stop! You should hear the names going around about me" Crapalotty" and "Thunder Botty Lottie" being some of the kinder ones" continued Lottie. It's just awful" she cried.

To be honest I did then start thinking up names in my head myself "The fountain of sluice" came to mind, but then I realised this was bad news, how would I get the know about the Council view on Little Hampton humping now!

I told Lottie not to worry, and advised her to get a lawyer. "You could get a fortune in compensation, for the stress of this". I proclaimed

But Lottie just wanted to get back to work. I arranged to meet her in a couple of days for a coffee and a chat at the "Coffee and Drop in Café" in Snobihill. Although now a few of the letters are missing so the sign now reads "Coff and Drop Café" Emily thought it was a medical centre!

Another mission now. Get Lottie back to work. The sooner she's back the sooner I get up to speed regarding the humping. Otherwise it could be the last time we ever get up to any speed in Little Hampton High Street.

Tuesday 13th January

Foggy all day

Another trip this morning to the Two Stop Grocery store. When I arrived, Mr Khan was busy stacking shelves. For some reason I started singing "Stacker Khan let me tell you what I want to do. Do you feel for me the way I feel for you? Stacker Khan let me tell you what I want to do." I thought it was funny as did Mrs Rogers who was in the shop at the time. But Mr Khan just looked at me, and then stated that he was a married man. "To be honest I'm surprised at you and whatever you want to do please keep it to yourself Mrs Ramsbottom, and no I do not feel the same way" he whispered to me." This is a respectable shop" he continued.

There was no point explaining as he obviously had no idea who Chaka Khan was, so I just paid for the milk and left. Fine start to the day.

I met Wendy Miller, on the way home, Wendy has poor vision she is a neighbour who has lived in Little Hampton from the age of five, I assume she must now be in her eighties. Wendy always walks as if she is fighting against the wind, almost at a ninety-degree angle. It's as if Wendy is in a terrific hurry but nobody has told her feet! Her guide dog Oscar very patiently walking with her at a snail's pace. Oscar is a Golden Labrador who is also getting on a bit himself, in dog years he is probably older than Wendy. Oscar had his paw bandaged which he lifted to show me. "Is he ok" I enquired " "No he is not"said Wendy "His eye sight is failing and he accidently knocked over my jam jar full of drawing pins and then stepped straight onto them, he has so many pins in his paw he sounded like he was tap dancing as he was jumping about on my wooden floor, the poor thing" said Wendy. "It took the vet half an hour to extract them all" she explained.

"Is that safe, having a Guide dog that can't see?" I enquired. Wendy explained that she had had Oscar for thirteen years and couldn't bear to be parted. It was very sad. Oscar and Wendy hobbled off trying to avoid obstacles as they went.

Surely, she should have another dog, or a guide dog for

the guide dog.

Emily phoned this evening to ask me to if I wanted to join the local slimming club, to be honest I hadn't thought much about it, but after the speed dating incident, perhaps losing a few pounds might be a good idea. Also if Emily could lose a few pounds then the car horn tooting may recede.

Emily seemed very excited "It's a cake only diet" she exclaimed. "It's run by Marie Anne Tornet" she said. "It's called "Let them eat cake and lose some weight". This seemed ridiculous. "You have to be joking" I said. But Emily had spoken to Veronica Boniton at the Bridge Club and she had lost three stone in as many months. She did say she was joking about the organisers name, I had stupidly believed her.

"It's on a week on Wednesday evening at the Village Hall at 7.30pm, Veronica said next week is Battenburg week" Emily said with so much enthusiasm It was hard to refuse.

I somehow have now been talked into this and will be accompanying Emily.

Wednesday 14th January

It's a lovely sunny day but very cold.

I went for a walk this morning as it is such a lovely day. Not many people about this morning.

I checked the Village Hall notice board and noticed that Monday evening there is a Drama Class. "The Wee Dram Theatre Group". The Drama group meet every Monday at 7.30pm. It said it welcomed everyone. They need people for the Summer Farce called "Back Side Story".

I have always wanted to be in Am Dram, so thought I would give it a go. I phoned Emily and she agreed to join me on Monday. She said "Her Lady Chatterley was legendry in the school play". If I remember rightly her body stocking caught on Mellor's (played by Jimmy Shuttletons) snake belt in what was supposed to be a very tame love scene. The snake belt ripped the body stocking from top to toe. The school play ended up being a lot raunchier than the book, and that had been banned!

The situation was only saved by two stuffed Rabbits hanging in Mellor's shed and Mr Riley the Deputy Head throwing his Trilby onto the stage for Emily to cover her modestly. She still insisted on taking a bow before being ushered off the stage.

With so much going on this year I thought I had better open the Calendar bought for me last Christmas by the Major, although I was reluctant to open it as it was called "Sixty Shades of Grey". I remember he sniggered as he gave it to me on Christmas Eve. "I saw this and thought of you" he said as he handed me the present wrapped up. He then left laughing.

I opened it only to find that each month had five shades of grey at the top with the dates below, I did smile, but still wasn't sure if the Major knew what was in it, or what he meant by "Thought of you?"

Thursday 15th January

Freezing!

I went to Leamington today and met Lottie Thatcher. Lottie was too embarrassed to meet me in Snobihill in case she bumped into anyone from the Council. We met in a secluded tearoom just off the High Street. It is called "Loose and Perky!".

 I assumed it was referring to the tea and coffee and not the Lady that runs the establishment!

Lottie was already sitting at a table when I arrived, immaculately dressed in a tweed skirt and cashmere lilac twin set, with matching gloves. I noticed her hat and hatpin on the table. You would have thought she was going to Ladies Day at Ascot races. I felt very underdressed in my New Look pink blouse and Primark cropped denim trousers.

Lottie was still upset, but she had contacted a Solicitor. "I went with Derek Death of Life and Death Solicitors, I would have preferred Leonard Life but he was scuba diving in Florida". Said Lottie

I had seen the advert for them in the local library "If it's a matter of life and death, it's a matter for Life and Death Solicitors". Not very catchy.

Lottie said she had a strong case against the Council as they obviously had no proof it was her at all.

"Derek Death or Death as pronounced when saying Teeth." said Lottie "He had advised her to have a stool sample ready just in case it is required for analysis in her defence. Just the thought of it has made me extremely constipated" Lottie explained. "Now my irritable bowel has started up again" she whispered in dismay.

To be honest the fruit scone I had ordered might as well have gone back, as it was becoming less appetising as the conversation went on, after listening to every detail of Lottie's past motion and her struggles on the toilet seat.

I did try to make light of it by saying, "I bet you couldn't even manage to put the word "Save" on the wall with the amount of excrement your churning out at the moment" unfortunately I said this a little too loudly and I noticed a few tuts as cakes were being pushed into the middle of the tables around me.

Lottie just looked at me in horror, I was not sure if her red face was due rage, embarrassment or just the constipation.

Sadly, Lottie's return to work did not seem to be imminent, so the humping progress at the Council cannot be monitored at the moment.

We left the Café and Lottie went home in a bit of a huff. I did a bit of shopping and bought some yellow wool just in case it was a requirement at the knitting circle.

Watched TV this evening, what a load of rubbish! Started watch a programme how to save electricity.

I took their advice fifteen minutes in and switched the TV off, although half way through the programme was probably not what they intended!

Friday 16th January

Heavy Rain all day

Stopped in this morning due to the weather, thought about washing my nets but read a book instead.

This afternoon I had to venture out as it was the Knit and Natter meeting, I'm sure the time is going quicker it seems to go faster each year.

The knit and natter group was thin on the ground this afternoon, Jane Roid was there checking everybody's daffodils, I produced my twenty Poppies, to looks of amazement.

You would have thought I had entered the room naked by the looks I was getting,

Thankfully Mrs Catterack arrived with a bright yellow balaclava and Mrs Beaverbrook had made thirty-five yellow egg cosies.

Jane Roid went mad. "Does nobody listen?" she shouted. "Daffodils. Daffodils. Not Poppies, Balaclavas or Egg Cosies. What good is a Yellow Balaclava to anyone." She continued.

Then as if she wasn't annoyed enough fellow knitter Veronica Sheppard walked in with a Casserole dish. We knew she was arriving because you could hear her hearing aid whistling long before she walked in the door.

"What have you got there?" asked Jane Roid. "It's a Madras Curry for the Hospice like you asked for" Veronica announced.

"I didn't ask for any such thing" said Jane Roid. "Yes, you did you said, nick some Daffodils. Well I certainly wasn't going to do that so I tried to buy some and you said make a Madras Curry! Well I couldn't get any Daffodils because there not in the shops yet and there is nothing in my garden either, so I just made the Curry" said Veronica.

Jane Roid scratched her head, and then the penny dropped. "I said knit some Daffodils for Marie Curie, not nick some daffodils and make a curry" she said in dismay.

Jane Roid sat down in a chair said she needed younger people in the Knitting Club, preferably people who can hear.

"I suggested that the name didn't lend itself to younger people, the Little Hampton on the Rise Knitting Circle sounded like a club for the elderly. "I suggest we changed the name of the club, to something dynamic" I said. Jane Roid agreed.

Suggestions were not in abundance, "The Crafty Knitnees" was an early suggestion by me, but after the blank response it was turned down, "The Knit Wits" said Mrs Beaverbrook.

We decided to have a cup of tea and open our Black Magic chocolates. "I only come for the chocolates" said Mrs Catterack. This got me thinking "The Black Magic Knitting Circle" the thought of chocolates always attracts people of all ages" I said. Everyone agreed and then Mrs Beaverbrook said she would put an advert in the local paper. We shall await the new members.

At this point Mr Tway arrived. "Sorry I'm late he said but I had a call from my friend, he was in a right state, his Twingo had been rear ended." It certainly lightened the mood!

We managed twenty Daffodils before calling it a day.

Saturday 17th January

Damp and Cold

I do hope this weather cheers up it has not been a great start to the year.

Emily phoned this morning to see if I wanted tickets to see Fred and Sid at Snobihill Theatre. I had never heard of them. "Fred and Sid who?" I enquired. Emily then said "You remember Fred and Sid from Opportunity Knocks! They came fourth when Peters and Lee won it in 1973." I was none the wiser. Emily went on "Don't you remember Hughie Green saying "Now if you want to vote and you can't spell Fred and Sid just write Glockenspiel and Euphonium on a postcard and we will know who you mean!"

"They had that legal battle contesting that the Clapometer was rigged. Surely you recall that? Said Emily

I was more concerned about the act, it didn't sound very good. But once again Emily persuaded me it would be a good night. So Emily decided to book the tickets for next Saturday at 7.30pm.

I can't say I am looking forward to it, they must be in their nineties at least.

Emily told me to "YouTube" them, I did and immediately knew I had made a mistake. "Chirpy Chirpy Cheep Cheep wasn't their best choice, but it was the only one posted on YouTube.

It was awful, I tried to phone Emily back, but before I had chance to dial the phone rang it was Emily to say she had bought the tickets online and she would see me Wednesday at the Village Hall for the Cake Diet.

I am beginning to think Emily is losing the plot, or I am for agreeing with her.

Later that afternoon Mr Littlemast from the Council phoned to ask if I would be able to stand in for Henrietta Plomb the Lollipop lady in the next village, "It should be the Monday morning only, as Henrietta has got an appointment to have her ...." Mr Littlemast paused "her Do Da looked at, if you get my drift" he said sounding embarrassed.

Not having a clue what he was talking about, I found myself saying " So old H-bomb has reached that age has she, of course I will cover, I assume her Lollipop Stick is still in its usual place, or has she had an accident with that, and that's why she has the appointment"

To which he replied after a long silence "Yes it's behind number tens dustbins" and put the phone down.

Being on the Lollipop Emergency supply team, is another string to my bow. Emily sometimes calls me Dorothy as she says I'm a member of the Lollipop Guild!

Sunday 18th January

Brass monkey weather!

Winnie the Pooh Day. Not sure what I should do so I had some honey on my All Bran.

Up early as I thought I would go to Church this morning, partly because of rallying the troops for the Humping campaign, partly because I needed to get closer to God, it had been a while. Mainly though to stop Father Aweigh from coming to the house as I hadn't vacuumed or dusted, also I had only just bought some Chocolate Hobnobs and I would like to eat them to myself.

I walked there, togged up in my boots, long black overcoat, woolly hat and a muff to cover my hands. As I approach the Major was at the gate talking to Father Aweigh.

"Morning Ramsbottom" the Major shouted as I approached "I see your dead cat has been given an airing, I haven't seen that a while" he continued pointing at my Muff. I started praying earlier than I thought I would, praying he would shut up.

Father Aweigh looked on embarrassed. "Morning Ophelia, nice to see you, I hope your better?"

No idea what he was going on about, I replied "Much better, thank you" and went into church.

As I walked in, Mrs Jacobs the Church Warden said "You look well?" "Yes, I'm fine Thank you" I replied.

Mrs Jacobs then looked to the church roof and cried "Praise the Lord".

After a further five people asked me how I was feeling, I suspected something was amiss.

Then I opened the Church News Letter to find my name top on the prayer list for the sick?

To my horror my picture was on the "Light a Candle for this Person" table and below my picture was about thirty lit candles. I've no idea where the picture came from, but by my expression on the photo I wouldn't have given myself long to live! I looked so much the worse for wear on it.

Father Aweigh then started the Mass with us all giving thanks for Mrs Ramsbottom's unexpected recovery. Stating that only last week he had had to visit me as I was too weak and frail to attend Church.

There had obviously been some mistake, but what do I do?

In the end I said nothing, but the fact that so many people cared and prayed for my well being brought a tear to my eye. It was like attending your own funeral. I know, everyone attends their own funeral but you know what I mean. The fact is these people some of which I hardly know cared about me, and that was a lovely feeling. This is why I said nothing, this doesn't happen to me very often if at all.

When everyone had gone, I removed the photo and lit a

candle myself.

I stayed there for a long time watching the flames dance, contemplating on where the last seventy years of my life had gone. Then I had a twitch at the back of my nose and sneezed very loudly, blowing out every candle on the table. I hope this isn't symbolic!

Monday 19th January

Colder than yesterday but the sun is shining.

National Popcorn day, just as National Obesity Week has finished!

Very cold last night, I needed an extra blanket under my candlewick bed spread.

This afternoon Emily and I are going to the Drama class at the Village Hall but this morning duty calls.

I donned my white coat and hat and set out for Cottage in Arden the next Village along from Little Hampton and their Primary School Saint Drogo's. Why name a school after the patron saint of unattractive people. What message does that send out to the pupils?

He is also the patron saint of coffee houses, does Costa really need a patron saint?

Anyway, I was a bit short of time when I arrived but fortunately the Lollipop was in its usual place so I picked it up and got straight to work, crossing the children and parents on their way to school.

After a half an hour I realised I was getting some funny looks. One driver shouted "What's happened has the Dentist upset you" out of his window and laughed as he passed me. I had no idea what he was going on about. Another shouted "Careful you might have a brush with the law" he also laughed and drove off. I had no idea what was going on, I thought perhaps I had some Alpen stuck on my teeth.

I was just coming to the end of the shift, when I noticed my Lollipop had been tampered with, it read "STOP CHILDREN FLOSSING". Why didn't anyone say? I felt such a fool.

This evening I met Emily at the Wee Dram drama school, but there was a sign on the door stating that the meeting had been postponed until Thursday, due to five thespians going down with something after visiting an authentic Thai the weekend. I can only assume it was a restaurant?

Emily enlightened me "They are rehearsing for the farce "Back Side Story"", the rival gangs are called the Shirts and the Vests, it's a parody of Sharks and Jets remember in West side story?"

I did remember, Thursday will be intriguing!

Tuesday 20th January

Cold, Windy, Snow Flurries.

A right old day, up early and the heating wouldn't come on, I am freezing.

I phoned the gas company who said that they wouldn't be able to come out this morning, but as I was old, they would try and make this afternoon. One benefit of being over seventy.

The day got worse, I decided it was probably warmer out than in, so I togged myself up and ventured to the Two Stop shop as I needed some eggs and flour, just in case I had to make a cake for the Slimming Club. I met Wendy Miller on the way and poor Oscar her Guide Dog now had a bandage on his paw and a nasty two-inch gash right in the middle of his forehead.

"What happened to Oscar?" I asked Wendy. "He walked straight into the edge of the kitchen cupboard" said Wendy.

Such a shame, but then matters got worse. Wendy said she needed a tin of beans and I said to save her coming in the shop with the dog and risk him knocking everything over I would get them for her.

Wendy waited outside the shop by the door, Oscar sat patiently next to her with his bandaged paw held up and the gash on his head.

Father Aweigh arrived at the shop and thought Oscar

was one of those charity plastic dogs for the blind, he then tried to push a fifty pence piece right into the gash on the top of poor Oscars head.

Oscar let out an almighty yelp and bit the Priest on the leg. Oscar then ran off straight into a lamppost and knocked himself out.

Wendy was pulled over and fell into the bin outside the shop. Father Aweigh was hopping around calling for Mary, Joseph and the Lord himself.

It was pandemonium. I rush out with the tin of beans still in my hand which I hadn't paid for only to find myself being apprehended by the new overzealous seventeen-year-old security guard that Mr Khan had employed on work experience.

It was at this point to add to my embarrassment Jane Roid drove past in her car. Just as I was being frog marched back into the shop. "Let her go, you idiot" shouted Mr Khan to the security guard.

After what seemed to be an eternity, we managed to get Wendy out of the bin, thankfully she seemed ok.

Father Aweigh was still hopping but had quietened down, he went into the shop where Mr Khan got a packet of plasters off the shelf and put one on Father Aweigh's leg.

The Priest was not very impressed when Mr Khan gave him the rest of the packet of plasters and asked him for £2.45.

Poor Oscar was still out cold and the Vet had to be called. It was at that point I came home.

I will get the eggs tomorrow now. The Gasman never turned up.

Wednesday 21st January

Thankfully the wind has eased somewhat. The weather that is!

National Hug Day, who thinks these up? I will give it a go later.

A weird day, making a cake to take to the slimming club seemed a very strange thing to do. But that is what I did this morning. I baked a lemon drizzle. Then I remembered Emily saying it was Battenburg week, I don't expect it will matter.

Emily arrived lunchtime with Fish and Chips in her hand, "I dropped in at Load of Cods Scallop" announced Emily. Load of Cods Scallop is our nearest chip shop. "Think of it as the last supper" she said even though it was far from supper time as it was only 12.30 in the afternoon.

"Anyway" continued Emily "The heavier we are at today's weigh in, the better we will look next week!"

We played Scrabble this afternoon in spite of the outburst last time. I manage to add the word "contem" onto Emily's word "plate" which made the word "contemplate" on a triple word square and won the game. Very pleased with that.

This evening we walked down to the Village Hall, I handed over the lemon drizzle to the organiser Patricia Lardy. Not the best name for running a Slimming Club. Her attire consisted of a bright pink very baggy valour tracksuit her hair was a similar colour. Patricia could be six or sixteen stone you really couldn't tell.

By the look on her face you would have thought I had placed a lump of dog poo in her hand. "What's this? Lemon drizzle week was two months ago" she sighed and put it on the table behind her.

A good start I thought.

The pink one then spoke "Right everyone form a queue it is time to weigh in" The twenty or so slimmer's formed a queue, not all seemed happy, some looked very nervous.

Your weight was only stated if you had put weight on, this worked as an incentive apparently.

The Pink one then tutted loudly as she looked at poor Mrs Hardcastle and then at the scales, "Sixteen stones eleven pound" announced Patricia to the group, Mrs Hardcastle walked away in tears, it was quite brutal.

Emily and I got on the scales not together obviously.

Whilst Emily was on the the scales, Pat checked her

weight, she then tutted loudly gave a heavy sigh and entered Emily's weight into the "Black Book! I thought Emily was going to explode she was so annoyed.

The diet was then explained to the group "Battenburg Week, replace four main meals with a one-inch slice of Sainsbury's Battenburg" said Patricia.

Hardly rocket science.

We then bumped into Wayne, Gail's Nails husband. "How ya doing Mrs O, yam here for the diet or just the cake" He said laughing. I smiled while trying to signal to Emily to head for the exit.

He continued, "It's brill this cake lark, I've lost a stone, most of it off me arse which is strange"

He then turned for us to look. He went on "I tell ya I had an arse like an umpalumpa three months ago, it's great ain it"

To be honest he still had.

Home at 8.30. Emily tooted as she left, while braking at the T junction. The day that stops I will know the diet is working!

Thursday 22ⁿᵈ January

Frosty and very cold

Gasman arrived this morning. Two days late!
Apparently, my flue needs some attention.

He then said "My internal thermostat was also up the
swanny" I don't know why I replied with "Welcome to
the world of the menopausal woman" but I just said what
I was thinking.

It didn't seem to matter as there was no re-action, he
only looked about twelve, so I don't think he had a clue
what I was talking about.

Also how many young people say up the swanny,
perhaps the Gas board have a list of descriptions to
choose from when things go wrong, and drill those
sayings into the young apprentices. At least he didn't say
it had "conked out" altogether!

Two hours later I had heat, thank goodness. It was the
first time I had been warm for days, I then remembered
it was Am Dram day!

Emily arrived after tea and once again we made our way
to the Village Hall.

The Director of the play Everard Tudor-Pole was very
welcoming. I guessed he was the Director as he was the
only one wearing pink trousers a yellow velour shirt
with blue braces. He immediately had me cast in the
role Maria's mother. "Can you just say "America" for

me darling?" he asked me.

"Can I take my coat off first?" I asked "Just say it darling, just say it" he replied

"America" I said after clearing my throat. Everard looked at me with his fingers on his chin deep in thought "Not enough conviction darling but we can work on that, practice that for next week" he said. He then turned on a sixpence at walked off.

Everard was then on the stage. "Attention everybody" he commanded clapping his hands.

The thirty or so people turned to face Everard.

"Now I want you all to get into couples, I want you all to practice furtive glances at each other for twenty minutes" stated Everard.

Emily and I did not have a clue what he were going on about, so we followed the others.

Then we had to mime the "Lord's Prayer" to each other, that was tricky, how do you mime "Hallowed be thy name"? Finally, we had to eat an imaginary packet of crisps and our partner had to guess if we were enjoying them or not.

Everard walked amongst us, while this was going on. He looked at Emily, his fingers on his chin again, "I sense you don't like Cheese and Onion?" he said to Emily who was pulling the most hideous face.

"How did you know?" Emily replied sounding surprised

"Darling this is why I am the Director" Everard replied.

Emily and I deserved an Oscar for keeping a straight face and not laughing.

Everard was back on-stage commanding attention again. "You!" he said pointing at Emily "I see you as Policewoman Officer Krapknee" Emily replied "Don't you mean "Officer Krupke"?

"Back Side Story, it's a farce Darling go with it. See you all next Monday as usual" said Everard who then disappeared quicker than the shop keeper in Mr Benn. What a weird day.

Friday 23rd January

National Pie day

Typical my heating is fixed and we have the hottest January day for sixty-five years.

Strange day today, very warm a neighbour told me that Wendy Miller had been stung on her nose by a wasp. How unlucky is that women, a wasp sting in January.

The meeting is arranged this evening for the "No Humping Campaign" led by Emily and my good self.

I printed off forty leaflets explaining the proposals by the Council which I had taken from their Website.

I am not at all sure what I was going to say this evening

and already the nerves were setting in.

Gail came over to do my nails, "Yow should see the commotion yam sturred up, the Village is more split than the ends of me air" said Gail while painting my nails "Winston Green"! Gail had some strange colours in her nail varnish pallet.

Stuart Delaney the local environment expert text to say he couldn't make it as he was at a Health and Safety convention in Pontefract for the weekend, shame he would be very useful but at least he is on our side.

The meeting was well attended, it was good to see Wendy Miller and Oscar who now both had swollen faces! Not so good to see was the Major. I reckon about thirty-five to forty people had turned up which was good news. But the evening didn't go as planned. Firstly, nobody reacted to my joke when I said "My Goodness, I have never seen such a dense crowd!". I heard one woman mutter "Bloody cheek".

Then the key to the room with the chairs couldn't be found so everyone had to stand.

Emily and I stood on the stage, and asked for ideas and concerns from the floor. This went well enough, Fumes, the noise as cars went over the humps, Father Aweigh was worried about his cars low exhaust, and Wendy was concerned about the humps being tripping hazards, these were all very positive concerns. Then someone suggested getting some T-shirt's made with a slogan on the front. We said these were very good ideas and thanked everyone for their input.

I then asked for a Committee to be set up. That's where it all went wrong!

 "I am happy to be Secretary but I do need someone upstanding in the Village to be the Chairman". I announced

The crowd below now seemed to have bunch up nearer the stage, then Mrs Ravensbrook who has a wandering eye said those immortal words "Will you stand Father Aweigh?" Mrs Ravensbrooks one eye looking at the Priest but the other was looking at Mr Tway, who was standing next her. Mr Tway immediately responded to her request and took a step to the side and stepped on the Major's in growing toenail. The Major jumped up shouting something I can't repeat but it preceded the word Idiot. He fell backwards knocking over six people. From the stage it looked like someone had triggered Domino Rally, by now twelve people were on the floor, three of which were on top of Wendy and Oscar. Within ten seconds only five people were still standing.

To make matters worse Mr Jenkins was stuck under all sixteen stone of Mrs Hardcastle, the lady I met at the slimming club. Mr Jenkins is the Editor of the local newspaper. I am dreading seeing his "Hampton Bugle" next week!

One lady was out cold for a few minutes, she woke up in a right panic as Father Aweigh was attending to her when she come round, she thought she was receiving the last rites.

An ambulance was called as two ladies couldn't get up. The meeting was adjourned as everyone seemed to helping everyone else exit the building. Fine start to the Campaign.

I must say the Japanese Brandy was very tempting when I got home, but thankfully I resisted.

Saturday 24th January

Still warm and sticky in January!

I had to make a few phone calls this morning to see if everyone was ok after last night's debacle.

All was well apart from a few bruises, except for Mrs Catterack who had her hearing aid pushed a bit too far into her ear by Mrs Ravenbrooks stiletto. The hearing aid had to be removed under local anaesthetic but she seemed ok and most people found the whole incident amusing fortunately.

I had a day in today as this evening Opportunity Knocks, if only!

I am going to see Fred and Sid at the theatre with Emily this evening. Can't wait!

Emily picked me up for another embarrassing trip into Snobihill a lot of braking and tooting along the way as Emily is less confident driving at night.

When we arrived at the theatre the place was almost deserted. After having a coffee we entered the auditorium. We were on row F but to be honest we could have almost sat anywhere.

The lights dimmed and a very frail sounding voice came over the loudspeaker, "Ladies and Gentlemen put your hands together for Fred and……" There was then a lot of coughing and wheezing before we heard the word "Sid".

"I hope the staff have checked the Defibrillator is working" I whispered to Emily

Well you can only imagine what it was like, a Euphonium and a Glockenspiel playing Goldfinger as their opener, followed by Copacabana and surprisingly Frankie goes to Hollywood's Relax.

Sid then took a breath from his Euphonium and had a puff on his inhaler before they started up again. "Now that your all in the mood, we are going to play that great Glen Miller classic". Sid announced.

We both settled back for "In the mood" but they start playing Rhinestone Cowboy by Glen Campbell.

After which Sid apologised saying "He always gets those two mixed up"!

In the interval I googled the pair Fred is eighty-seven years of age and Sid ninety-two.

The Interval had taken well over half an hour when a

message then came over the loudspeaker "Due to unforeseen circumstances there will be a delay to the second half". A paramedic arrived and disappeared into the theatre. We had no idea what was going on.

Eventually we took our seats for the second half and Fred and Sid appeared to rapturous applause. "Don't worry everyone" said Fred in a very strong Yorkshire accent " We are both in fine fettle, but sadly one of our most ardent fans was overcome with pains in her chest ironically when we were playing "Don't go breaking my heart" at the end of the first half" he continued " We would like to wish her well, and dedicate this next number to Doris, hoping she has a speedy recovery"

They then started playing Wings "Live and Let Die" which didn't seem very appropriate under the circumstances.

I think "Live and Let Die" was a little bit too ambitious for the pair. Sid was a red as a beetroot by the end of it. His inhaler was in excessive use once again. Fred too was mopping his brow profusely.

An hour later the show closed with their Opportunity Knocks number from 1973, Chirpy Chirpy Cheep Cheep. Which resulted in a standing ovation, both Emily and I felt oblidged to stand as there was only about thirtyfive attending the concert, all of them had got to their feet.

Home later than expected at 11.30pm with Chirpy Chirpy Cheep Cheep ringing in my ears until I eventually got to sleep at 2.35am.

Sunday 25th January

Freezing this morning, no wonder we catch colds.

Burns Night!

I went to Church this morning it is very quiet, the congregation was down in numbers too. I heard that most of them are unwell. More to the point everyone thinks that I have given everybody whatever I had last week.

I wanted to tell them that I didn't have anything wrong with me, but what could I say.

I didn't even know what they all thought was wrong with me.

I then had to light twenty-five candles one for each of the congregation that were ill. There were so many photos on the candle table it looked like a game of Guess Who!

Father Aweigh said "Perhaps I had been premature in my return and he thought I should go back home and rest"

Home by 10.45am. Kicked out of my own church!

I spent this afternoon in my house, recuperating from the illness I never had.

I had a phone call this afternoon from Jane Roid, there is a spare ticket at tonight's "Burns Night" at the village hall. So I said I would have it.

Jane Roid said "There's no dress code but wear something Tartan".

I have nothing in Tartan, so spent the rest of the afternoon looking through my entire wardrobe, the only thing I could find was a Bay City Rollers Scarf which had been left behind by my Niece when she visited me in 1975. For some reason she never wanted it back!

I arrived at the village hall wearing my Bay City Rollers scarf around my wrist, well it wouldn't fit around any other part of my anatomy. The Major greeted me at the door, he was dressed in more Tartan that a Vivian Westwood fashion show, he was proudly wearing a very large sporran. The Major looked me up and down and said "Shang-a-Lang" in the same vein as Lesley Philips used to say "Ding Dong".

I ignored him and walked in. It wasn't a bad night, lots of dancing and live music. Mr Khan then paraded the Haggis which was piped in by local farmer Mr MacDonald on his bagpipes. That would have completed a good night if Mr Khan hadn't dropped the Haggis which knocked a very hot toddy out of Jane Roids hand scolding her arm. She had to be taken A&E, but finding somebody sober enough was a challenge. In the end it was Mr Tway who took Jane to the hospital as he announced he had only had a single Virgin Daiquiri all night? It's a mocktail apparently!

Burns night had certainly lived up to its name!

The Haggis was devoured by Oscar as it rolled under the table right under his nose. It's the first bit of luck that dog has had in a long time.

Monday 26th January

Gloomy and cold

Drama day again, every day seems to be drama day.

Like a fool I did spend some time in front of the mirror saying America over and over again and tried to dress in the correct attire for the part of Maria's mother.

Emily arrived dressed much the same in a tight hooped blue and white top a little bit too tight if you ask me. We sat down for lunch and we both had our one-inch slice of Battenburg as prescribed.

Emily then produced a yogurt out of her bag, "This is desert" she announces defending herself.

Later we ambled down to the village hall to the Drama Group.

As soon as we walked in Everard met us both. He was dressed in black lycra from top to toe, with a bright yellow baggy jumper over the top. He immediately stuck a large orange square sticker on my breast and a large silver star on Emily's. Such was the placement of Emily's sticker she looked like she had come straight from the lap dancing club after a rough night.

"Groups darling, get in groups. Em you look for fellow silver stars and you" Everard said pointing to me "You're with the squares"

He then leaped onto the stage like a panther, clapped his hands and announced "Groups get into groups" ordered Everard to the crowd below. He then explained what the day held. "Squares think Depression, Tri-angles think Fragile, Circles think Empathy, and Stars think Gratification." He then clapped his hands again to quieten everyone down. "I want you to talk in groups and improvise a three-minute play based on those emotions in ten minutes time"

He then jumped off the stage and shepherded us into four corners of the room.

Thankfully most of my group were well on the way to depression already, they were a right miserable lot.

We were up first and decided to be mourning the loss of a loved one in our play. Mr Tway was in our group and surprised us all by bursting into tears as he reflected on the death of his goldfish Tarquin who had passed away in 1967. The group just consoled him, as he was sobbing like a child. Everard loved it "Excellent Darlings excellent." I knew Mr Tway and he was the most unanimated man I know. I still don't know if he was acting or not!

Emily over milked her Gratification play, I have never seen anyone so grateful at being given a fusty

Fisherman's Friend to suck on. But once again Everard was clapping his hands with joy.

Before going home Everard assembled us all on the stage and gave us all a song sheet. The song was called "I'm so Witty". Everard went to the piano and started playing the West Side Story classic "I'm so Pretty" in a more flamboyant style than Liberace. "Sing for me my angels, sing" he ordered. Well the lyrics left something to be desired. Think of anything vulgar rhyming with witty and you had the next four verses. If only I was as confident about this farce as Everard is.

Later this evening I had a phone call from the Major informing me that Stuart Delaney had died last weekend. He had slipped on a banana skin and hit his head on a discarded mop bucket at the Health and Safety Convention in Pontefact.

It is such a shock.

Tuesday 27th January

National Story Telling Day!

The doorbell rang at 8am, it rang again at 8.01am and 8.02am. I eventually got up. It was a parcel delivery, the parcel wasn't for me, it was addressed to the Major. He had instructed DHL to deliver to my address as he may not be in. I signed and took the parcel from a young man whilst trying to keep my modesty as the wind battled with my dressing gown when I opened the door. At ten o'clock the doorbell rang again, thankfully I was dressed as it was the Major who had come to collect his parcel, he had been in his house all morning but couldn't be bothered to get up to answer the door. What a cheek. I was tempted to hit him with the parcel, but it had fragile stamped all over it. "Have you treated yourself?" I enquired "No, no" said the Major "It's a do it yourself Vajazzle kit for Mrs Tushingham" she was too embarrassed to have it delivered to her house, in case it was obvious what it was from the packaging." He explained. I wasn't sure he should be telling me this.

It was only when he had gone that I realised I had received the package she was too embarrassed to receive. I was so annoyed.

Jane Roid phoned again this morning asking when the next Humping meeting is, although I think she really rang to give me some gossip about poor Stuart Delaney.

According to Jane Roid, Stuart was a Health and Safety course last weekend with Miss Clutterbuck who works at our local bakery "Dreggs". "Now it could be all above board, but she has been seen giving him an extra-large portion of Lardy Cake every Tuesday for months" said Jane Roid.

Jane Roid then mentioned his reputation and an episode a few years ago between Stuart and Ms Gladstone who worked at the Corn and Callus our village pub!

"Then there was the liaison with that Cassandra the lady he met at the Poundland bargain bin" exclaimed Jane

"She had succumbed to his charms before you could say Jack Robinson".

"She had only popped in for some bin liners" said Jane raising her eyebrows.

"The list goes on and on. He was also on the verge of divorce apparently and no wonder, I think his wife Desdemona Delaney had had enough" Jane continued.

I had no idea all this was going on. Jane said she suspected foul play and thought he may have been bumped off. A ridiculous notion but it did make me think.

Wednesday 28th January

Grey with a deep depression until lunchtime, the weather that is, although it could be me!

I looked in the mirror this morning and thought "Mirror, mirror on the wall who is the fattest of them all". The only thing that cheered me up was finding a slice of Battenburg in the cupboard.

This afternoon it was that dreaded Slimming Club again. Emily arrived for lunch thankfully she hadn't been to the chip shop, so we had pilchards on toast and pickled onions. Emily said "If the Pink One announces my weight today, I will breath all over her, that will bring a tear to her eye."

We played scrabble before going to S Club. Emily

thought it was funny putting ARSE from the A in the word LARD I had previously played. I was too nervous to appreciate it.

Once again we arrived at S.Club and were notified that next week is Swiss roll week. It's ridiculous, how can this possibly work. Emily and I watched in horror whilst the Pink One announced one weight after another. The women were being led away in tears. We waited our turn with trepidation.

Emily kicked off her shoes and approached the scales in a very confident manner. It felt like an age and then nothing was said the Pink One just smiled and entered Emily's weight in the book. I then approached the scales of doom. The digits on the scales flickered from one number to another, it was like waiting for the Grim Reapers scythe to fall.

Amazingly I had lost a pound thank goodness, it was probably due to the stress of it all but unbelievable all the same. Emily then admitted to me that last week she had put the weights from her Victorian kitchen scales in her underwear, as she wasn't taking any chances, she still had a two-pound weights in her bra this week, unfortunately she had put them both in the same bra cup. I was amazed there was room but it did explain her listing to one side when she walked.

The Pink One then got up onto the stage, "Ladies and Gentleman" she announced "Can you please put your hands together for this week's biggest loser! This lady has lost an astonishing six pound in a week! This is a

club record. The lady who has worked marvels is Emily"
Everyone clapped and Emily just took the applause with
gratitude. What a fraud. She even went on to explain
how she did it, Battenburg twice a day apparently!

I was praying for the weights to fall out when she took a
bow, but there was little chance of that. Those weights
wouldn't have budged if she had done a handstand!

Thursday 29th January

Sunny but cold.

Well at last we have some good news this year. Lottie
Thatcher phoned to say after her solicitor Mr Death had
contacted the council, she is able to return to work next
week.

Apparently, the council HR had another incident to
investigate when the words "Save our Pensions" were
written in excrement again in another ladies toilet.
Obviously, this is what the protester intended the first
time but the culprit must have run out after writing
"Pens".

I presume this time they must have stored it up
somewhere or ate an awful lot of bran the night before.

So Lottie is completely exonerated, as her stool sample
didn't match the excrement on the wall and she wasn't in
the building when the second incident occurred. I would
have thought Lottie not being at work would have been

enough to prove her innocence.

"The culprit however is still at large" said Lottie "Militant Martin the cleaner is now prime suspect, as no-one believes a woman would do such a thing."

Who needs Midsummer Murders what with this and the Stuart Delaney mystery, I think we are living it?

Mr Death the solicitor is still seeking compensation for Lottie for the humiliation and stress of it all.

But the good news is, one, she is still speaking to me and two, I can now get some information on the humping issue direct from the Councils mouth.

Friday 30th January

Sunny and very cold

Franticly knitting this morning as it is Knit and Natter day, I have only made ten daffodils in the last fortnight. Jane Roid will go mad.

Pat the postman knocked on my door this morning, I had a letter I had to sign for.

It was a Christmas present from my penfriend Debbie who lives in the USA.

Better late than never I thought, after all Christmas day always creeps up unexpectedly!

I was annoyed because I had sent her present in November to make sure that she got her Eskimo mittens on time. I completely forgot that Florida was eighty degrees this time of year, but it's the thought that counts.

I opened the present only to find a box containing a pressure sensor aid for the elderly. You put it under your mattress and the bedroom light comes on if you get up in the night. Not sure if I liked it or I was angry that she thought I was incapable of turning a light on.

This afternoon it was the Knit and Natter meeting, it's really just an excuse for a gossip.

There was a right commotion when I arrived.

A Policeman was the club, he was talking to Jane Roid, who was shaking her head and looking very concerned. We were all very worried and thought it might be to do with Janes daughter Emma who seems to be in trouble all the time at school.

He then asked Mrs Beaverbrook to join them. This went on for about half an hour then the policeman left.

Jane Roid then asked us to gather around and gave the explanation.

Mrs Beaverbrook had put an advert in the Local Two Stop window and another in the Hampton Bugle regarding the Knitting Club and our new name. This should have read "The Black Magic Knitting Circle" unfortunately it didn't!

There had been several complaints to Mr Khan and to the Police, also Mr Jenkins the Hampton Bugle Editor had also received a string of complaints regarding Mrs Beaverbrooks advert that she had placed in the paper. The reason for this is the advert read as follows. "The Black Magic Circle meet at 2.30pm every other Friday afternoon at the Little Hampton Village Hall. Don't worry if your new to this, needles will be provided" Sadly Mrs Beaverbrook had omitted the word Knitting. You can imagine the hoo-ha that was generated in the Village. We will never live it down. Matters were made worse when two new potential members arrived and left when they realised it was a Knitting Club and not the Black Magic Circle. That was quite disturbing.

So not much knitting done today and certainly no chocolates.

Saturday 31st January

Sunny

Today is my Brother Peters birthday he is sixty-eight years old. That seems ridiculous as it only feels like minutes ago that I was taking him to school.

I had a walk to the Two Stop Shop this morning. Mr Khan started singing "That old black magic has me in its spell" He found it funny as did the customers in the shop at the time. I suppose I will have to put up with this for a while.

Mr Khan then went on, "I know you didn't mean any harm Ophelia, you have always had a soft centre" he again started laughing.

Then to my horror the Major walked into the shop, "Morning Ramsbottom" he said "How are you?"

I waited for the quip but there was nothing. The Major then said" If you need any help, or anyone gets on your nerves just let me know." I was amazed. I thanked him for his concern.

I left the shop very confused. The Major had turned my Black Magic moment into the Milk Tray advert. For one second, I was quite moved. Then I thought, what am I doing this is the Major!

I went home for lunch and had tomatoes on toast, and then went into Snobihill this afternoon as I decided to get some new clothes. Well that was a waste of time that was. Why is it the elderly have to wear bright flowers, frilly cuffs and elasticated waists. New Look was a little bit too new for my liking. Marks had nothing in to my taste. I eventually found a lovely fitted blouse in dark navy, it was for sale in a little boutique just outside John Lewis called Vettements de Merde. The attached label said reduced by seventy percent. I got quite excited until I saw the reduced price of £275. Originally £640. That's crazy. I told the assistant as much too. She wasn't very impressed. I did say to the other customers excuse my French before leaving.

I picked up the spring edition of "What's On" from the Theatre Box Office before coming home. A complete waste of an afternoon.

Sunday 1st February

Gloomy, ghastly and glum with a gail force wind.

White Rabbits, I have no idea why people say that, but better to play safe.

The big decision today was whether to attend church or not. I was up early due to the terrible wind. The Majors downpipe had kept me awake, it definitely is in need of some attention, it was making an awful noise most of the night.

As I was up early I decided to go to Church. The Church was packed when I arrived as it was a Baptism, there must have been three hundred people attending.

Normally it is fifty at most.

A strange Baptism, it was twins being baptised but both the children were at least nine years old. Sapphire and Duke banged each other's heads while arguing over who was going to be baptised first, then Sapphire dropped her "Lime Fruit Shoot" into the font. The font itself was then knocked over while they both scrabbled to retrieve the drink, this soaked poor Mrs Beaverbrook who was holding a candle for Father Aweigh. Her cassock was in a right state. It was probably just as well the font had been knocked over as the holy water had taken on a strange shade of green.

This was eventually sorted out with Sapphire and Duke duly being made Christ's children. I'm sure Christ was well pleased!

A woman at the back of the Church then asked if her son could be done while Father Aweigh had the font out. Father Aweigh was completely taken aback by this and rightly refused.

Well what a commotion pursued. A giant of a man stood up and shouted "I ain't leaving till my Aston Martin has been Christened".

That confused matters, when Father Aweigh stated that as much as he loved cars they can't be Christened. The whole thing got completely out of hand. The font was knocked over for a second time. Half an hour later Aston Martin Donnelly the man's son was christened very reluctantly by both Father Aweigh and Aston himself who almost screamed the place down.

Sometimes it's better to stay at home.

Fortunately, the rest of the day was quiet, the wind had also calmed down.

Monday 2nd February

Warm rain.

I had scrambled eggs on toast for breakfast this morning, that was a mistake. Within the hour my stomach looked like I was seven months pregnant, unfortunately I knew it was going to erupt at some point.

It did, half an hour before Emily arrived to go to the Drama Class. It was very embarrassing. "Bloody hell it's a bit heavy in here" she said as soon as she walked in. She then opened a window "What have you been eating" she then said "Don't tell me" she paused sniffed the air and said "I'm getting curry, cauliflower and scabby dog" It wasn't funny, I had to go to Drama Class in less than an hour.

After being jet propelled all the way to the Village Hall, my wind eased fortunately. Emily and I walked in, again we were greeted by Everard, who handed us both a pair of marigold gloves.

Everard was wearing pink dungarees over a loose-fitting red shirt embroidered with daffodils. He didn't have Marigolds on, he wore blue velvet evening gloves.

"This week I want to cover the art of seduction" he announced. "Darlings I want you to take the gloves off and set my heart racing"

We all looked at each other very puzzled. Everard then jumped up onto the stage and proceeded to demonstrate.

Well I can't say it got my heart racing, it was funny though as he tried his hardest to look seductive, pulling each finger of the glove off with his teeth. He then threw each glove into the audience. He finished and took a bow whilst we all applauded.

Then it was our turn, well it was ridiculous, how can you make marigold gloves seductive?

We tried though, the trouble was getting the damn things off. Emily was almost sick as her gloves were very smelly and it was only when she had tried pulling them off with her teeth that she noticed something green stuck on one of the fingers."

"Not a great success, but well done for trying" said Everard. To finish we had to sing the "Maria" lyrics again as provided on a sheet by Everard. Once again, the lyrics had been changed, the opening line was now "Diarrhoea, I've just had a bout of diarrhoea." I can't believe I am a part of this.

Everard jumped up on the stage again clapping his hands "Next week we are casting, so think about the best part that suits you" He said as he gave everyone a list of the parts to be cast, He then bowed and left the stage. He is a very odd man.

Emily's name was already on the list, she had been cast as Officer Krapknee.

Tuesday 3rd February

Spring is in the air, it's eleven degrees

The phone rang this morning it was Emily reminding me that this evening is the Charity Quiz Night, it's a good thing she reminded me as I had totally forgotten.

We had been badgered into this by charity organiser Richard Boe at a Rotary Club Christmas bash we had attended early in December. It is in aid of Richard and his wife Bo's Charity "Children in Weed". I'm not sure if it is to do with drugs or gardening as I bought the tickets for tonight's Quiz just to shut Richard up as he was boring me rigid at the time. I do recall him saying the charity name was Bo's idea. "You would be amazed how many donations we get online during "Children in Need" week. My wife has become quite adept at changing the N to a W on the cheques we receive by mistake." Richard proclaimed. I wasn't sure this was ethical? The Quiz tickets cost £80 a team so it had better be good.

Fortunately, I managed to get four of us together to make a team, so at least this spread the cost.

Our team consisted of Emily, the Major, Jane Roid and my good self. Heaven knows how the Major ended up in our team, I must ask Emily how that happened.

Emily arrived at 4pm with an M&S meal deal. We polished that off and an additional bottle of wine by 6pm.

Jane Roid picked us up in her Renault Clio at 6.30pm, Thankfully I got the front passenger seat, the Major and Emily in the back. My seat was so far forward my head was touching the sun visor, it was still a feat getting the two of them in, being a two door didn't help. "By god Gal this is a squeeze" said the Major to Emily. Finally, we got my seat down and the door shut and we were on our way. I looked over my shoulder to have a chat and could barely make out where the Major was, I could only see his head and his bright red nose. Emily seemed to be lying across him.

Well it was another disastrous night, when we arrived, we noticed everyone except us were wearing dickie bows. I read our tickets, Dickie (Richard) Boe requests that everyone wears a dickie bow, anyone failing to do so must pay £5 to the "Children in Weed" charity. As it was my fault, I felt obliged to pay the £20 for the team as none of us donned a DB. The Major looked Bo the organisers wife up and down, she was also dressed in her Dickie. He then asked Bo if she had ever worked at the Playboy Club, she just tutted and walked off.

We found our table and then had to think up a team name, after much deliberation we agreed on Three Nubile Nymphs and a Nutter. We thought it was funny. The Major gave our team name to Richard who was on the stage.

The ten team names were then read out by Richard for Bo to put on the overhead projector before the Quiz started.

"The Surgeons, The Accountants, The Pharmacists, The Barristers, The Snobihill Scientists, The Poets Society, The CEO's, The Politicians, The Lecturers, and finally Three Nubile Nymphs and a Nutter."

If that wasn't embarrassing enough, we then had to answer the questions. The first round was in Latin!? Not surprisingly the Pharmacists and the Barristers were leading after round one, we had zero points.

It didn't get any better in round two, Noble peace prize winners of the nineteen fifties. There were lots of nodding heads all around as the questions were asked, our fountain pen was still waiting to be used.

The following rounds the main ingredients of Malagasy Cuisine, that had the same response. Sport got the Majors hopes up until the questions were announced name the ten members of the 1988 Winter Olympic Canadian Curling Team. Again, everyone's pens were scribbling away.

We ended the night feeling very stupid, we had one point, we only got this because Jane remembered that Edward Heath had a dog called Erg in the World Prime Ministers Pets Names round.

The Barristers won it with nintyone points out of a hundred, all the other teams scored over sixty.

We made a very quick exit. Home by 11pm. Emily stayed over as she had had too much to drink to drive.

Wednesday 4th February

Winter returns it's Freezing

Not much going on this morning, starting channel hopping and found an interesting vet program called Get Set for the Pet Set Vet Set, it was about how they attend to animals with broken bones.

I have never seen a Canary with its leg in plaster before, I wasn't sure the little boot he had on was really necessary.

I have never been so bored.

This afternoon is the monthly U3A meeting, this month's talk is something to do with cheese, I can't really remember. Anything has to be better than daytime television.

As I left the house I was greeted by a strange smell in the air, it reminded me of sweaty socks. Not pleasant at all. The smell got stronger and stronger as I approached the Village Hall, then it dawned on me. Cheese!

I arrived at the village hall early for a change, the smell was over powering. Jane Roid took me to one side to tell me when Stuart Dellaney's funeral is taking place, she looked like she had been crying but I think it was due to the stench of cheese!

The funeral is at eleven o'clock a week on Friday, so she is moving the Knitting Circle to another date as she will be going to the funeral and thought a few others would too.

We settled down to listen to our guest speaker Peter Pringle. He informed us that his talk was called "Ticklemore, Lady Jane and the Stinking Bishop" I did wonder if I was at the right lecture!

Jane Roid looked very embarrassed when the Major piped up, with "Blimey Jane you kept that quiet!" Peter Pringle quickly informed us that there was nothing sinister in the title as they are all types of cheese.

I think a few of us including myself were a little disappointed.

On the table in front of us were about thirty different types of cheese, the front row held hankies to their noses as the smell was so overwhelming. Peter talked about his life and fascination with cheese it was mildly interesting if not lengthy, he went on for an hour at least. He then asked the audience to name their favourite cheese. You could see the disappointment on Peter's face when Mrs Catterack shouted out Cracker Barrel almost at the same time Mrs Beaverbrook shouted Dairylea.

He then asked anyone if they fancied tucking in to his Slack Ma Girdle. I'm sure he was winding us up, but there is was on the table with the rest of the cheeses.

 I haven't seen so many blue veins on display since the ladies over sixties water aerobics class at the swimming baths. I did play safe when tasting the cheese settling for a small wedge of Double Gloucester.

The Major however was like a child in a sweet shop, tucking straight into the Slack Ma Girdle, this had somehow been impregnated with a piece of Sinking Bishop, the Major got more than he bargained for as Stinking Bishop is a very strong cheese. His head went so red I thought he was going to explode.

"By God that's got a kick" said the Major. Peter advised him not to go straight into Slack Ma Girdle better to try some Ticklemore first"

"That probably explains why your still single Major!" said Jane Roid who had been waiting to get her own back all afternoon.

Home by 5pm, but could not get the smell of the Stinking Bishop out of my nose, it wasn't until much later that evening that I found a piece of it in my pocket. I bet that was the Major's doing.

Thursday 5th February

Sunny but cold

I was quite optimistic this morning the sun is shining it is crisp cold but a lovely day. Not much going on today so I thought I would get around to doing some housework.

I was vacuuming the hall when Mr Jenkins Hampton

Bugle appeared through the letter box.

To my horror my picture was on the front page above the headline "Local Knitters in Voodoo raid"

Also on front page there were six photos of members of the Knitting Circle, Mrs Beaverbrook, Mrs Catterack, Jane Roid, Mrs Andrews, Mr Tway and me. We looked like members of a vicious gang of organised crime. Mr Tway was wearing a patch, I have never seen him in a patch in my life.

I was shocked to say the least, my photo was the same hideous photo that appeared on the candle lit prayer table at Church. Where does that picture keep coming from?

I continued to read the article, the next headline below "Local Constable probes Jane Roid"

I thought I had jumped to another story for a minute!

It then read Circle Leader Jane Roid held for an hour by PC. Mrs Beaverbrook also quizzed.

After many accusations on the front page all true but with the typical Bugle sensationalism the story continued a page twelve. It was only there in a very small column that the mix up was explained and our innocence revealed.

I decided to stop in to avoid embarrassment, the phone never stopped ringing though, some phoned just to ridicule me some to sympathise. Emily was one of the former, she found it hilarious calling us the Little

Hampton Six.

Jane Roid rang she was distraught. So she should be, on her photo she had a huge blond perm, she looked like a negative of a young Michael Jackson. On the plus side she did look younger.

Mrs Andrews was most upset, she had only popped into club to donate a couple of balls of double knit and said she would sue the paper.

Hopefully things will soon be forgotten, I think the Editor Mr Jenkins was still upset about the debacle at the humping meeting a couple of weeks ago and that's why he published the article, he still has bruises from that night apparently.

Friday 6th February

Foggy

A nice quiet day pottering around the house. I started reading a new book "The Art of Relaxation." I got very frustrated with this as I was three chapters in and it was still rambling on about how to get in touch with your inner self. I had to put the book down otherwise I would have thrown it out of the window!

Gail arrived this morning to do my nails, no sooner had I let her in she was off "Yam going to that Gigolo's funeral next week?" questioned Gail. I assumed she was referring to Stuart, before I could answer she was off again "The things I heard that man has done, he was a right one, I can tell yer"

I waited to hear what exactly he had done but she didn't tell me. Instead she produced her latest colour in her emporium of nail varnish bottles. "It's called Simply Red" said Gail. That was strange as the nail vanish she was holding was blue. "It's blue" I informed her. "I know it is now, but yow should see it a night! It's bostin ain it"

I was already buffed, manicured and ready so I gave it a go. It's definitely blue!

This afternoon I picked up the Art of Relaxation book again, Chapter six suggested soaking in a bath with oils and candles. My last two attempts at this were a disaster, the Bath Bomb incident in January and the incident in December when I applied the thimble of scented oils as directed and the top come off the bottle, half the contents of the bottle went into the bath. I got in alright but getting out was a nightmare, if you can imagine Scooby Doo swimming that must have been what I looked like. It took me half an hour to get out.

Hence the book is back on the shelf never to see the light of day again.

My Mother would have been a hundred and five today, I say this every year, she died fifty-two years ago. Still miss her terribly. She had a hard life working in the Cotton Mills in Lancashire from the age of fifteen years old which probably explains her premature death. Her favourite line was "Don't be so bloody daft" I think this to myself so many times lately and for so many reasons.

Saturday 7th February

Cold and damp

This afternoon is the Jan Gough painting class at the village hall, I am quite excited as long as the Major doesn't make another appearance.

I arrived early as I wanted to set out my paints.

Jan Gough announced that today we are painting portraits. The first hour we practiced and Jan advised us on our technique, then she handed out a picture to each of us which we had to paint as best we could. I was handed a picture of Humpty Dumpy. "Is this right?" I enquired "Yes, but try to make him look angry" replied Jan!

That was a waste of time, he looked more inquisitive.

"The second hour was quite exciting" Jan announced. "The nine painters should get into groups of three as we are competing against each other, like Portrait Artist of the Year on TV".

Jan said each group of three would paint a member of the Village who have kindly given up their time to sit for us this afternoon.

"Not the Major again!?" shouted Bernadette making the

sign of the cross and looking to the heavens.

"That's one member, we don't want to see again" said Mrs Hargreaves

"Certainly not" Said Jan quite shocked. "These are all respectable ladies"

The three ladies then appeared and sat on the seat provided in front of three artists each. The models being Mrs Ravensbrook, Wendy Miller, Miss Everton. Not the best people to paint.

Wendy's Glasses are thicker than any bottle end, Miss Everton was wearing a balaclava and a snood with it being so cold, you could only see her nose. As for my sitter Mrs Ravensbrook she had a wandering eye.

My contenders were Bernadette O'Leary and Harriet Hargreaves, I felt quite confident until I saw Skinny Frank the chip shop owner turn up, we don't call him skinny to his face because he is quite the opposite. He was helping Jan judge our work? Do I now regret moaning about his portion size last year?

It wasn't a bad effort in the end, I made sure both Mrs Ravensbrook eyes were looking very left, unlike Harriet who just went for it, and painted as it was. She won as well because Jan liked her Picasso style.

Picasso my backside that's how she looks!

Sunday 8th February

Sunny again

Well I thought I was going for a walk this morning and then a nice pub lunch this afternoon with Emily, that was until ten minutes before Emily was due to arrive.

I noticed to my horror the words Betty Darver's Mother on the calendar!

Betty Darver is a fellow lollipop lady who I cover for when needed, I used to go for a drink with Betty many years ago and also knew her Mother.

Betty had called me the other day to say she was away for a four-day weekend in Yarmouth, apparently Donny Lonegan the Lonny Donegan Tribute is appearing on the pier this weekend, Betty was a big fan of Lonnie's "My Old Man's a Dustman". Anyway, she wants me to look in on her Mother who must be a hundred at least.

She is in the Sunset Care Home and I agreed to look in on her today to put Betty's mind at rest.

Emily and I had a very short walk and a sandwich at home. I then went on my way heading for the Sunset!

Getting in the was an ordeal, security was intense, a photo ID had to be produced that took an age, a password and door code to remember, voice recognition test and then verification of my identity by my driving licence. Finally, my retina was scanned. Thankfully they didn't do a full body search.

Then I was escorted in and taken to see Clara Darver, Betty's Mother. What a waste of time, she had no idea who I was. She thought I had come to mend her mobile phone, "I can put the numbers in but it won't dial out" Clara shouted. To kill some time, I asked to have a look at it. Not that I would have a clue how to fix it. Clara rummaged in her bag for five minutes and the handed me her mobile.

"There's a very good reason why this isn't working I informed her, it's a calculator!

She then insisted she had spoken to her Daughter on it only last week. I had a right game convincing Clara otherwise. We never did find the actual mobile in spite of searching for an hour.

The Carer then informed me that she didn't have a Mobile. What an afternoon.

Then I had a terrible time convincing everyone that I was visiting and not a patient. They had put my details in wrong when I arrived. Thank goodness for that retina scan otherwise I may well still be there. Half an hour later I got out just in time to see the real sunset.

Monday 9th February

Freezing cold

I ate my porridge and watched Lorraine this morning by the fire, it is very cold today. I can't say I am looking forward to going out to Drama this evening.

Later Emily arrived with a huge bouquet of flowers and a card, "Happy Birthday" she said as I opened the door. All very nice but I said to her "It's not my Birthday" Emily looked at me "Are you sure?" she enquired. As if I didn't know my own birthday.

"You did exactly the same three years ago it's the 9th of March" I informed her. She finally agreed with me and said I might as well keep the card, she then put the flowers back in the car!

We togged up and ambled down to the Drama class.

Everard met us at the door, looked us both up and down and said "Well you obviously didn't get my text" he then said "It's dance week darlings, I've swopped my directors head for my choreography head this week"

This explained why he was dressed in a lemon leotard over lilac legging and pink leg warmers, he looked like a chicken.

"You two should be in Lycra, how can you both be expressive in thick woolly cardigans?"

He then twizzled around, clapped his hands and commanded that all the group watched his moves. It was funny, Everard arms were waving about as he leapt like a Gazelle across the floor, finishing his routine kneeling in front of Emily with his clasped hands thrust forward under her nose.

He then put the "West Side Story" score on the laptop and we got into two groups and pranced about for half an hour and running towards each other clapping our hands. As directed by Everard "Practice, practice, practice darlings" he demanded.

"Now have you thought about casting? Oprah what part do you want to be?" he said pointing at me.

"The part of Anita in West Side Story" I replied ignoring the Oprah mistake. His fingers went on his chin while deep in thought, he then put the music to America from West Side Story on the Laptop. "Here's the lyric's my angel, sing for me" commanded Everard.

So I sang best I could with his lyric's "I like the smell of formi-ica, I like to sit on formi-ica, ev'rthings free on formi-ica, I'm out my tree on formi-ica!

"Very good" he said "and it's A Knitter not Anita in this play."

So I have the part of A Knitter, I am thrilled it is very rare that get any accolade, in fact I think it is the first time, never being told you are any good at anything does bring with its low self-esteem.

I was so thrilled I phoned Peter (Titan) to tell him. I told Mom and Dad too, just hope they can hear where ever they are. I went to bed this evening and shed a tear. It is funny that even at my age you still want to tell your parents if you achieve anything. I whispered "goodnight love you" to myself before going to sleep!

Tuesday 10th February

Frosty

Went for a walk to the Two stop shop this morning. The Major was in there deep in conversation with Mr Khan. "I say Ophelia can you tell me the name of the Shakespeare play with McDuff in it?"

"Macbeth" I replied The Major and Mr Khan went into a fit of giggles. "Bad luck old Gal" said the Major. "I thought you Thespians couldn't say Macbeth"

"Very funny" I replied. How fast does news travel in this village. Then I thought to myself, I hope it isn't bad luck. I bought the milk and was just about to leave when Richard Boe walked in with his son Harry.

"Hang on, I have something for you from the quiz" said Richard. He then went out to his car and returned holding a five-foot wooden spoon. "You hold this for a year, it's the prize for coming last."

He then bought his son a packet of Haribo's, not even realising the irony! Richard and Harry Boe then left the shop. I am now left standing in the shop holding this monstrous spoon.

Mr Khan said "You can use that when you stir the Cauldron in the play, what's it called?

"The Scottish play" I said smiled and left carrying the spoon home.

I had ordered my main grocery shop from Waitloads a

few days ago which was due this afternoon. My two-hour slot came and went. The shopping arriving an hour later. The delivery man Nigel announced "Sorry for the delay, but I had to make a detour due to my dodgy bowels this afternoon. A word of advice Treacle, don't go for an Edwina at the Haji Bhaji on a Monday night!"

He then thrust a bag under my nose "Here's your fresh fish." I found it amusing, that a man with a mullet was delivering mullet.

I put the shopping away only to find the delivery note stating that two items were not available so alternatives have been provided. The Chapstick had been replaced with a cream for cracked nipples, and my natural yogurt had been replaced with a tube of Canesten!

I'm going to look a right Charlie taking those back for a refund!

Wednesday 11th February

Sunny

I awoke in a sweat this morning, after yet another nightmare, this time it was a giant pink swiss roll chasing me over a cliff.

I then realised to my horror that it is the dreaded Slimming Club this afternoon. I didn't go last week because of the U3A Meeting. Although I did get the nod from Emily that it was Jaffa Cake week last week.

I avoided breakfast and then cleaned the house from top to bottom in a vain attempt to burn some calories. By the time Emily arrived I was in a right state, I needed a shower, as Emily confirmed as soon as I answered the door.

I missed lunch and watched Emily tuck into bread and soup. Emily informed me that the last of the kitchen scale weights had now been removed from her underwear, so this week she should be ok when she steps on the scales. She will probably be Star of the week again!

We arrived at Slimming Club, as we walked in the Pink one was arguing with Wayne. "Yem Scales are bosted, I ain't put on tow pounds" proclaimed Wayne.

The Pink one looked flustered, this was a first. "I assure you my scales are correct" replied a very pink Pat Lardy. It was like watching Gladiators.

Wayne wasn't giving up "I'm telling yow there's no way this arse is any bigger than last week. The only thing Lardy is yow" he proclaimed lifting his Donkey Jacket displaying his rather large posterior.

Emily whispered to me "Now that's what I call a super moon", I assume she was referring to its size.

It was Emily who intervened and asked Wayne if he was wearing different clothes last week.

"Perhaps if you removed your Donkey Jacket" she suggested trying to be diplomatic.

But Wayne wasn't happy "I always wear me DJ for weigh in. A bloody week of Jaffa cakes for this!"

He continues his rant "Yow can stick a Jaffa up your lardy arse, I've ad enough" he shouted at the Pink one.

Wayne then stormed out.

The Pink One was very upset, she sat in a chair being consoled by members of the group.

Thankfully I lost a quarter of a pound and Emily half a pound, which was lucky as she had taken a pound weight out of her bra. She should be half a pound heavier. Belgium Buns week this week my favourite, so this is going to be a challenge.

Thursday 12th February

Cold and miserable.

The humping prevention campaign has to be re-ignited after the last disastrous meeting. So I booked the Village Hall for the first Tuesday in March.

I phoned Lottie Thatcher this morning to see how things were going at the Council. The Phantom as he or she is known as now, is still carrying on making a statement on the ladies toilet wall.

The last one stated "How's this for a lump sum" said Lottie "Although this one was smeared and not as solid" she continued. As if I cared! "At the moment it is still being treated internally" said Lottie.

"As should the culprit" I replied to which there was a silence "Perhaps it's a smear campaign" I said but again there was still no response. Then Lottie said "Sorry Ophelia I have to go, it's the monthly stationery stock take" With that she put the phone down.

That aside I did get some gossip on the High St humping in the Village. Work is planned for June 14th, so I have got a few months to get some support.

Emily dropped in later for a game of scrabble bringing with her fish and chips, she said that there was a right to do in the "Load of Cods Scallop" Chip Shop. Apparently because they are now using beer batter on the fish and cider vinegar on the chips, so you now have to be over eighteen to buy them.

Emily seemed flustered "Well I thought there was going to be a fight when baby face Terry Toowlin the Geordie was refused to be served, just because he didn't have any proof of age. I'm sure he is in his thirties.

The chip shop Manager Skinny Frank Poopalotapous was adamant, claiming it's a new EU directive". Said Emily.

"Mr Poopalotapous, does he have any relations who work at the Council!?" I enquired.

Again, no reply. A lot of tumbleweed moments today!

Scrabble was interesting. We decided to change the rules

and you got triple points if you put down the name of a fish. I scored sixty-six points for getting "Pollock" down. Although I did still so regret not using my letter B. Those opportunities don't come around very often!

Friday 13th February Oh No!

Cold but Sunny. Lovely date for a funeral!

It's Stuart Dellaney's funeral today, I don't think I have ever been to a funeral in the sunshine, so I wasn't sure what to wear. Jane Roid had informed me that it was a green themed funeral due to Stuarts love for the planet, what's wrong with black? Now I have got to look for something green in my wardrobe. I found a lime green twin set, and Olive-green skirt, there was a colour clash but it will have to do.

The Funeral was at 11am this morning so I donned my blue coat (I do not have a green coat but thought green and blue resembled the planet earth). I strolled down to the Church at 10.45am.

I arrived to be faced with a sea of black, no one was in green!

Jane Roid looked me up and down with a look of surprise. "I thought you said it was a green themed funeral" I said to Jane. "It is" she replied "He's having a wicker coffin!" Did I feel conspicuous.

Then I noticed the number of single women attending. It

was like the Grim Reapers beauty pageant.

All wearing heavy black lace veils so there was no way of telling whose face was behind them.

"No doubt that lot will be his lovers" said Jane nodding towards them.

There must have been at least thirty ladies.

As we walked into the Church Phil and Frank Enstien were handing out the Order of Service cards, they were both having an argument with a scruffy looking man.

The Enstien brothers now in their seventies always thought they were Little Hamptons answer to the Kray twins in the nineteen sixties apparently. They had both worked as Bouncers most of their lives.

Anyway, they wouldn't let this man in because he was wearing jeans. Another got refused because he wasn't wearing a tie. There was a right kerfuffle. Thankfully Father Aweigh come out and calmed things down.

Just then the Hearst arrived, and we all looked in disbelief at the sight before us. There was a wreath along side the coffin in the Hearse which read STUD in white carnations.

Apparently his work colleagues always referred to him a Stu D as there were two Stuarts in the office. So naturally that's what they had on the wreath they sent.

Then the black laced lovers started wailing, what a noise they made each trying to outdo each other.

The Service could barely be heard as the Lovers wouldn't give up.

We then went on to the crematorium. The coffin entered the crem to the sound of Tom Jones "Green Green Grass of Home", unfortunately it wasn't turned off at the end and we were also given the first few bars of "What's New Pussycat" which spoiled the moment somewhat, especially when Tom sang the lines "Pussycat Pussycat I've got flowers, and lots of hours to spend with you". This, for some reason sent the Lovers wailing through the roof.

Home by 3pm topped up with asparagus volovants and chicken tikka surprise. Hopefully the surprise won't be it reappearing later!

Saturday 14ᵗʰ February

Cold.

Valentine's day. I waited for the usual flood of cards to be delivered! To my surprise I had two, I know one was from the Major as I get one every year and the five lines are always a giveaway.

It read. **M**arigolds are yellow, **A**zealia's are bright, **J**unipers are blue, **O**phelia are you free tonight, I'm **R**eady and waiting for you. Not very subtle.

The other one however was a mystery, no more than a question mark and a kiss. The postmark was from

Norwich. I don't know anybody in Norwich.

Years ago, I had a holiday on the Norfolk Broads but that was in 1976. The hottest summer ever!

Only our boat could get beached forty miles in land, as the water on the Broads was so low.

Emily phoned later to say be ready at 7pm as she had a surprise, and wear something nice!?

Now what? I was now very nervous, but like a child I did as I was told. Dressed in a blue dress that would suit any occasion I waited for her arrival.

Sure, enough at 7pm Emily's horn tooted in conjunction with her brake lights. I left the house, not having a clue where I was going.

"Tonight, could change your life" Emily said as I got into her car.

That comment was none to reassuring, if she crashed the car that could change my life or even end it! I thought to myself.

We arrived thirty minutes later at a restaurant in the countryside. To my horror I noticed a sign "Valentine's Day Blind Date Night"

"You're not Serious" I said to Emily pointing at the sign. "Don't worry" she replied, "I submitted your likes and dislikes in men when I booked last week. For your hobbies I put Travelling, Hang Gliding and Russian History. It makes your look interesting and pretty much covers everything"

I was annoyed but did find it funny, not as funny as Emily though!

After a predinner drink Emily and I were escorted to our tables by the Concierge.

I sat there for about five minutes (It felt like an hour) before I heard the sound of footsteps behind me.

"Good Evening or should I say Dobryy Vecher?" said the gentleman behind me in a Russian accent. It was a good start as he sounded like Sean Connery if Sean had been Russian.

Sadly, this is where the resemblance ended, as I turned around to see a very large fair isle jumper and matching tie. His hair well, if it had been dragged through a hedge backwards it would have improved it. Boris Johnsons barnet was tidy in comparison.

"Good evening" I replied

I won't go into the whole night, but he was a perfect match! A perfect match having travelled the world, spending four years in Russia and had more than a passion for hang gliding.

I spent the whole night listening to his adventures bored rigid.

However, Emily was having a wonderful time with Eric the mime artist, who was her date.

It was a shame she couldn't mime her hysterical laughter, as the Manager had to ask her to calm down, she was so loud.

This was a mistake as nobody tells Emily to calm down, not when she has had seven gin and tonics.

She stood up and then fell over. Eric then imitated pulling on an imagery rope to try a pull her up.

It was funny.

Eventually they were thrown out. This took a while as Eric pretended to be fighting against the wind every time the door opened, he being blown back into the restaurant numerous times before being escorted out by two burly men.

This was good news as it gave me an excuse to leave. "Sorry I Moscow" I said to my date and left.

Emily though insisted on getting Eric's phone number before leaving, which she did.

I drove home. Emily and I sang "Born Free" only we sang "Horn Free" every time we stopped, all the way home.

Not a bad evening considering it was a disaster.

Sunday 15th February

Freezing cold but sunny.

The first Daffodil has made an appearance in my garden.

I decided to go to Church this morning after making sure there wasn't a Baptism.

The Sermon went on longer than expected, Father Aweigh droned on for forty-five minutes telling us why the Sermons should be kept thirty minutes long at most! Ten minutes in my mind had wondered to something else.

After the service I had a cup of tea, chatting as you do, when I noticed Mrs Beaverbrook was selling books. "Would you like one? enquired Mrs Beaverbrook "It's an "Old Testament Recipe Book" "Only £9, and proceeds go towards Mr Sodulot's operation to have a gastric band fitted."

Mr Sodulot was one of our regular parishioners until one day his budgie had a stroke. That was a shock to everyone especially Mrs Beaverbrook as she was very fond of Mr Sodulot's budgie. His budgie had always been so chirpy, you would often get a glimpse of it when Mr Sodulot got it out in his living room. After the budgie had had a stroke Mr Sodulot wouldn't leave it alone tending to his budgie each day. Instead of going out, Mr Sodulot ordered in "take aways".

As Patricia Lardy says at the Slimming Club "The faster the food the slower you get." Anyway, by the time his budgie had fully recovered Mr Sodulot was far too large to sit in our pews. This explain why I hadn't seen him for a while!

I felt oblidged to buy the recipe book bought from Mrs Beaverbrook. Actually I was intrigued, how much work and research must have gone into that book getting recipes from over two thousand years ago?

When I got home, I thought I might have a go at one of these aged recipes.

Well what a waste of time. Sacrificial Lamb Stew, Lamb of God Moussaka, Chicken in the Moses Basket to name but a few, and for deserts Adams Apple Pie and Jacob's Cracker Surprise!

Nothing aged about any recipe, even Noah's Casserole was a scam "Chop the vegetables two by two cm". was the only reference I could find to Noah.

Stayed in the rest of the day as it is very cold.

Monday 16th February

Black over Bills Mothers. (Raining)

My vacuum cleaner packed up today, but not before it decided to blow all its contents out instead of sucking just before it conked out. Dust was everywhere and no vacuum cleaner to hoover it up.

I went round to the Majors to ask if I could borrow his.

He helped me carry his very heavy Kirby Classic Omega which he had had since 1973.

He then left me with it and retreated from the scene. I started the thing up, it sounded like the Tardis in Doctor Who.

I took five minutes trying to prise the large vacuum head away from my carpet such was the extreme suction then the thing started pulling my curtains off the runner as I held it in the air.

I managed to swing it away from the curtains only to see my lace doily disappear from the top of the TV cabinet.

Before I could get to the plug to switch it off various things had rattled their way up the Kirby pipe.

I have no idea what was missing.

Back to the Major's house who couldn't understand what all the fuss was about." It's always fine on setting two" he proclaimed.

I returned to find I had it on setting ten, Turbo boost!

I'm sure he had set it to Turbo Boost on purpose.

This afternoon Emily and I ventured down to the Village Hall for the Drama Group.

Everard greeted us at the door, today he was wearing string vest and leather trousers. "The cast is cast" he said as we walked in "Today ladies I want your dark side"

Everybody had an envelope given to them, these contained the part they would be playing in the summer farce "Back Side Story". Emily was Officer Krapknee and I play the part of A. Knitter.

We then had to practice clicking our fingers to the beat of Everard's tambourine.

Then we had to practice whistling whilst clicking our fingers.

Finally, Everard demanded that the Vests went to one end of the hall and the Shirts the other.

He led the Vests as we approached each other. "I want distain for each other, give me distain" shouted Everard "I want venom in your eyes" he continued.

Fortunately, Mrs Tushingham was in the Vests group and I being a Shirt had no trouble showing venom in my eyes.

Emily said "What about Officer Krapknee?" to which Everard replied "Everybody hates you and you them"

Before we left Everard, announced that we should try and stay in character as much as we can during the week"?

I ignored Emily for the rest of the evening, and then explained to her that I was keeping in character! She hit me with a French stick!

Tuesday 17th February

Very Cold

Teeth chattering weather. I hope that stops as I have to visit the dentist this afternoon. I had a quiet but very nervous morning.

I hate going to the dentist even for a check-up, as was the case today. My dental practise is in the centre of Snobihill so I set out in plenty of time.

I arrived for my 2.30pm appointment. "Mr Sucregum has requested that all his patients fill in this questionnaire" said the receptionist as she handed me a clipboard and a twenty-page questionnaire. Questions ranging from "How often do you floss?" to "What is your favourite Ice Cream?" The final question being "Do your bowel movements smell of chocolate/cheese/fish? "please tick the nearest.

Lord knows what all that was about!

This took twenty minutes, as I handed it in I was called to see my dentist Mr Sucregum.

I lay almost flat in the chair with the light shining straight in my face. Mr Sucregum then started elevating the chair.

At that precise moment a dental nurse came in asking if Mr Sucregum could attend to a man in reception as a matter of urgency. The man had been rehearsing at Snobihill Theatre for tonight's show with the Kazoo

Ensemble when he tripped while playing "Strangers on the Shore" as a solo piece. He had lodged the Kazoo at the back of his throat. Now she mentioned it you could hear him from where I was lying. He sounded like Harry Corbett's Sweep but with a wheeze.

Mr Sucregum headed out of the room immediately forgetting that I was still ascending on the chair.

When people say at the end of their life a light comes towards them well that was happening to me only it was the dentists light as I was at least five feet in the air. I pushed the light away when finally, the chair reached its zenith and stopped. I was now lying about two feet from the ceiling, clinging onto the chair for dear life.

Fortunately, the Dental Nurse heard my cries and got me down. What a day!

To top it all I have to have a filling and go back in two weeks, Mr Sucregum apologised and said "He would waver the fee for putting me through such an ordeal."

As for Squeaky the Kazoo player, he was ok after the Kazoo was extracted.

It's a wonder Emily hasn't got tickets for tonight's Kazoo Ensemble performance after the Fred and Sid debacle I'm sure she would listen to anything!

Wednesday 18th February.

Sunny and Cold

I popped into Snobihill this morning to get a new battery for my watch. I dropped into "The Rocky Horologicalist" the new trendy clock shop. Unfortunately I arrived at the top of the hour.

Twenty clocks all chimed eleven o'clock at the same time, I now know how Quasimodo felt.

It was deafening.

Then as they finished chiming, "Rock around the Clock" blasted out from several speakers in the shop.It was so loud!

I shouted to the shop owner who was sitting crossed legged on a chair hanging from the ceiling. "My watch needs a new battery!"

He took the watch from me stared at it and said "This is a wind up".

"What do you mean a wind up? This isn't some joke, I need a new battery" I insisted I was quite annoyed.

"No, No, No, the watch it's a wind up watch not a battery" he said winding it and handing it back to me. I looked at the second hand making its way around the face of the watch. I felt so stupid and I had wasted my time.

I got home just in time to go to the Slimming Club with

Emily.

When we arrived, there were a lot of the members looking worried and rightly so. The weigh in results were terrible. Everyone had put weight on, Emily had put on four pound and I had put on two pounds.

The Pink One was going mad "What have you all been doing?" she shouted. She then removed reward star after reward star from the slimmer's star chart on the wall.

I then noticed Wayne had made a return "It ain us it's those bloody Belgium Buns, av you sin the bloody icin on those things, we ad no chance" he shouted.

"How many have you had this week?" she asked. "About twenty" came the reply from Wayne.

I though the Pink One was going to explode! But she just looked in horror and said nothing.

Next week it is Mini Swiss Roll Week and no more than one a day!

Thursday 19th February

Snowing quite heavy too!

What a beautiful morning white everywhere and that lovely dull quiet that comes with snow.

Unfortunately, I was in desperate need of bread. so against my better judgement I donned my pink wellies and set out for the Two Stop Shop.

Not a sole about due to the snow being about three inches deep. I was silly really going out.

The problem is that in my head I am still forty-one not seventy-one, everyone my age says the same.

I did however trace the neighbours who think it is ok to let their dogs foul the Village Green and not clear it up.

Their footprints and their dogs paw prints had left their mark in the snow. These prints led from their front doors directly to the dog poo and back again. The poo was easy to spot as the two tell-tale excrements were still steaming for all to see.

It was the new couple who moved into the village five years ago and surprisingly the other culprit was Father Aweigh and his Afghan Hound ironically named "Job" as both his and Jobs footprints led straight back to the Vicarage.

Not sure what to do with this information, I will have to give it some thought.

When I arrived at the Two Stop Shop Mr Khan had put up a sign "No Wellingtons" I thought he must have sold out which was strange as there was a row of them outside the shop. I walked straight in. "Get out, get out" Mr Khan shouted.

He did make me jump. "Can't you read?" he continued "It was like the great flood in here last year from snow covered wellies. Use the blue shoe covers and take those off," he said pointing at my wellies.

"It took me twenty minutes to get these damn things on and there is no way I am taking them off" I said as I picked up a loaf of bread slammed the money on the counter and walked out. Stamping my feet as I went.

I don't know what came over me, I think I was still annoyed about the dog poo.

Not such a beautiful day after all.

Friday 20th February

Raining, the snow has gone.

A quiet day today or so I thought. Nothing to do this morning, well that went to plan.

This afternoon it was the Knit Wits Knitting Club (Formerly known as the Black Magic Circle!).

When I arrived there all was quite normal, everyone had done their fair share of knitted daffodils for Marie Curie and all of us now saw the funny side to the remarks in the Hampton Bugle last month.

We were having our general natter while knitting, putting the world to rights as we do, when Jane Roids phone rang.

She looked very concerned, then said "Oh no, where is

she now?" Jane made a note and then put the phone down.

"It's Emma my Daughter, she's in Hurtglands Hospital A&E" stated Jane.

She could see by our faces that we were concerned.

"She was on the School Bus sitting on the back seat of the upper deck snogging Billy Shufflecock when both their braces on their teeth had somehow interlocked together. No matter how hard they tried they couldn't get themselves apart. They couldn't get off the bus for risk of falling down the stairs so the Fire Brigade were called. The Bus was evacuated. Eventually they were taken in an Ambulance to Hospital where they are now still locked together" explained Jane "Billy bloody Romeo Shufflecock! why him?" she muttered under her breath.

I said I would take her to the hospital as she was very shaken.

When we arrived, sure enough there they were in the corner of the A & E waiting room they looked like Rodin's sculpture "The Kiss".

Fortunately, as we arrived Emma's name was called, "Emma Roid?" enquired the Nurse. "No!" said the man next to her "It's just a rash I think!".

I had to look away as I had to stop myself from laughing, I had never thought about it before but why would you name your child Emma Roid?

Emma and Billy then shuffled like a pair of mating crabs across the waiting room following the Nurse into the cubicle accompanied by Jane and Billy's father.

Two hours later they emerged separated but both Emma and Billy looked like they had had botox injections such was the size of their lips.

I run Jane and Emma home, that was a long silent journey, so I put the car radio on.

What should be playing but Errol Brown and Hot Chocolate singing "It started with a kiss!", I soon turned that off!

Saturday 21st February

Sunny a nice day

It was such a cold night last night, how I miss someone to cuddle up to. It is all very well meeting friends but I have never got use to the empty house particularly in the winter.

Saturdays are always difficult as most of my friends are spending time with their families.

Even Emily is out today with Mervin the mime artist her new boyfriend. It's a pity he wasn't my date that evening as he seems a bundle of fun.

I have been freezing in bed and fed up with spending each night alone.

So I went online and found "Ted" described as a Non-Smoking, Non-Snoring, Non-Farting, and doesn't have boozy breath. He is six-foot-tall with a warm heart. He would love to share your bed every night.

This is just what I have been looking for so I immediately put in my details, hopefully Ted and I will be cuddling up on Monday!

Well that was one positive and something to look forward to.

As I had nothing to do today, I decided to visit my friend Albert. Albert goes to our church but I hadn't seen him for a while not realising, he was in Hospital, he too is in his seventies.

When I arrived at Alberts bedside, I noticed his dinner hadn't been eaten. I ask Albert if he would like anything to eat? To my surprise he said a McDonalds would be a real treat.

So I walked across to the McDonalds and bought him a "Happy Meal" to cheer him up. I had a Filofish thing, never to sure what I am doing in those places.

Albert was so pleased it made his day as he tucked into his meal. He even saw the funny side as he had had a blood transfusion only yesterday and his happy meal toy was a toy Dracula. We both laughed at that. Then sadly the humour was short lived as the Doctor came in to talk to him.

I said I would leave but Albert insisted I stayed.

The Doctor then stated his diagnosis. Half way through his "Happy Meal" Albert was told the outlook was very bleak. "Good job I didn't order an unhappy meal, only knows what the outcome would have been then!" said Albert trying to on put on a brave face.

It's so very sad. I left not long after as his family were due.

But it did put thing in perspective and made me realise how lucky I am.

Very excited about meeting "Ted" on Monday

Sunday 22nd February

Sunny again!

Up early a lovely day the sun is shining and all is well. It's amazing what a difference a beautiful morning can make to your mood.

I decided to go to Church this morning, completely forgetting that Father Aweigh had decided that today was going to be "Bring your Dog to Church" day.

It was like trying to get access to Crufts, where on earth did all these dogs come from? Father Aweigh stood at the gate with "Job" his beloved Afghan Hound by his side. Most of the congregation were new faces as were their dogs.

Well as you can imagine it was pandemonium.

Dogs fighting and barking, leads entangled but strangely when Mr Hardacre cranked up his organ so to speak, peace seemed to descend on the place and everything calmed down. It was either a miracle or Mr Hardacre's choice of music. He played "I Love my Dog" by Cat Stevens.

"Two things wrong with that choice of music, so there is" said Bernadette O'Leary who was sitting next to me "One his name has the word Cat in it, and two Cat Stevens isn't a Catholic!"

"Does it really matter?" I replied, "Just take in this beautiful moment"

The Service went well considering, Father Aweigh insisting that all the dogs came to the front and gathered around his Afghan Hound for a photo.

Even that was weird because all the dogs again were calm and looked at Job from either side.

It just looked like Leonardo Di Vinci painting of the Last Supper with Job the Afghan Hound looking the part as Jesus. It freaked me out a bit.

After the service I stopped for a coffee and spoke to a man I had never seen before Henry Dyson (The first man I have ever met who was named after two vacuum cleaners!) he had a coffee in one hand and a lead in the other with four doggy bags one hanging from each finger.

On the end of the lead was a "Cockapoo" puppy, a cross

between a Cocker Spaniel and a Poodle.

"That was a mistake" said Henry pointing at the dog. I misread Henrietta's Christmas list, she's my nine year old daughter. You can only imagine the upset-on Christmas day when she opened the present expecting a Cockatoo!

Looking at the bags on his fingers I said "It looks like he has the right name" pointing to the dog "It seems that all he does is cock a leg and poo!" This was greeted by a stony silence.

I left soon after as Mr Dyson was now swinging the bags around while talking and I was sure one was going to head in my direction at any minute. A nice day though for a change.

Monday 23rd February

Freezing

It is feeling very cold today. I stopped in all morning it is to cold to do any shopping.

Ted didn't show, very annoyed!

Later Emily and I went to the Drama Group. Everard who was dressed head to toe in beige suede greeted us at the door he looked very excited.

"Come in Ladies. Have I got a treat for you today" Everard proclaimed as we walk in.

When everyone had arrived, Everard leapt onto the stage.

Then he made his announcement "Well everybody I have good news, I now have a partner."

Everybody applauded not really knowing what else to do. "I hope you will both be very happy" I said

"No No No" he continued "A partner to help me directing this play!" he said going very red. In fact so red that with his beige attire he looked like a matchstick.

He continued "You may have heard of him? His Porgy and Bess was very big in Brighton"

We all looked puzzled.

"It's Dave Revel Tallwood the infamous Choreographer! announced Everard. Upon which a very tall man pirouetted onto the stage from behind the curtain.

Unfortunately, he caught his toe on a raised nail and tripped and nearly fell off the stage.

Thankfully Everard managed to grab the back of Dave's red braces and save him before he launched into a crowd surf.

Apparently, Dave is to direct us with our dance routines, it is getting very serious. We all have to practice twerking for next week!

Emily has got to put more effort into her truncheon swinging and make it swing to the beat of the music.

This is now at a whole new level from our earlier finger clicking and clapping!

Emily was far from perfect she had no rhythm what so ever, she was starting to resemble Charlie Chaplin the way she was walking with her truncheon.

I was glad to get home and in the warm. I did try practicing twerking in the mirror later that evening but it's not easy. I think I need a bigger mirror or a smaller backside!

Tuesday 24th February

Warmer today

I awoke in a sweat this morning so much so my hair was matted to my head and my nightdress was very damp. I thought I had a ringing in my ears too.

It was then that I realised the doorbell was ringing.

Who on earth would be calling at 7.15am?

I had no choice but to answer the door as I was. I opened the door to be faced by a seven-foot-high box, a hand reached around it and a voice said sign here, after which the delivery man jumped back in his van and left.

I was left struggling trying to drag the enormous box into the house, unfortunately the Major walked past with his Daily Telegraph under his arm.

"I say Rammy that's a nice box you've got!" shouted the Major at the top of his voice.

He then came over and helped me in with it. I didn't want to mention what it was as he would have thought I was mad, but unfortunately, he asked. "By gad Gal what on earth have you ordered?" enquired the Major. I replied with a stupid answer "A new vacuum cleaner" I replied.

"Bloody Hell Rammy, a vacuum cleaner that size, you had better nail your carpet down! Tell me when you're going to vac and I will tell the neighbours to keep their children in!" he replied laughing. I looked a right state and I just wanted him out the house. thankfully once the box was in the hall he left.

When the box was undone "Ted" appeared the six-foot-high Teddy Bear. After fighting to get him into the bedroom and onto the bed, I looked like I had run a marathon. He was much larger than I expected.

This evening it was the second Traffic Calming Prevention meeting. Thankfully this time we had a committee. Father Aweigh had agreed to be Chairman, I was Secretary, and Emily was the Publicity Officer. This time we had chairs and the meeting went without any disasters.

Mr Tway said he knew someone who could print some T shirts, so it was agreed to order fifty shirts with "No Traffic Calming Please on my Little Hampton!" printed on the front.

Also Emily was getting some posters printed and raising awareness around the village.

Very tired tonight so Ted and I had an early night.

Wednesday 25th February

Gloomy. Thank goodness its national chocolate covered nut day!

It's hard to believe but I checked there seems to be a day for everything.

I went to Emily's today for a game of Scrabble. I'm not keen on going there to be honest, her mugs are chipped and normally selected out of an over laden washing up bowl and swilled under the tap before making a cup of tea.

Quentin Crisp once said that if you stop dusting it doesn't get any thicker after four years. I think Emily's house is trying to dispute that theory.

Emily greeted me at the door and seemed very excited. The Birdy Song also greeted my ears, it was so loud I could hardly hear Emily speak.

Then she shouted three times "Alaska or I'll ask her" not quite sure which, then she boomed again "Volume two" fortunately the music then quietened down.

"Isn't it fantastic" she said pointing at the contraption on the table.

I knew it was new as it was the only thing that didn't need dusting!

"Any music you want to listen to, plus all your phone contacts" continued Emily

"Watch this" she said "Alaska phone Big Bottom" she shouted.

Sure, enough a second or two later my phone rang! "Big bottom!?" I enquired. "Oh, don't worry about that, that's the name in my phonebook it's a play on your name Ramsbottom" explained Emily.

Later after drinking my cup of tea from the wrong side of the cup as the other side still had red lipstick on it, we played our game of Scrabble.

While playing the game we were talking about the underwear at Marks & Spencer's in quite some depth, why wearing lacy underwear is a thing of the past, why we can't wear thongs anymore and how we now both need a gusset that can take a Tena Lady.

Just then we both heard a voice in the background "Hello? Hello? Is that you Emily" said the voice.

The voice was coming from the Alaska box "Hello who's is it?" ask Emily

"It's Mark, did you need anything?" he enquired. "No sorry it must have called you by mistake" replied Emily.

"Who's Mark and how long had he been listening to our conversation?" I enquired

"Mark's my Gardener, he tends to my shrubbery when the need arises" said Emily.

We then surmised that while we were talking about Marks and Spencer's it had called Mark.

Brilliant now everyone will be told about our underwear requirements!

Fortunately, we can see the funny side, which got even funnier after two glasses of Baileys!

Mark also knows more about Emily's shrubbery than he really wanted too!

Thursday 26th February

Cold and Raining

National tell a Fairy Tale day? That explains why the weathers Grimm!

Grim is the word of the day as today is the day I have to return to the dentist for my filling.

This morning I read the Hampton Bugle the headline read "Council Phantom Toilet Defecator, Police still have nothing to go on". This reminded me that I must phone Lottie and get the latest news.

I stopped in this morning and watched tv, that was a boring morning. I watched "Most wanted down under" it was about crime in Australia thankfully!

This afternoon I had another panic attack when I realised, I had to go to the Dentist.

I arrived and seemed to wait for ages listening to the drill whirring away in the distance which just cranked up my nerves.

Then my name was called and up I went to see Mr Sucregum.

He froze my mouth and while was waiting for that to go off, I developed hiccups!

It was so bad I had to go back into the waiting room until the hiccups finally stopped.

It only stopped because there was a promotional TV in the waiting room, before the video it started it announced that the following video had some upsetting images. It was a short clip called "Look after your teeth" It then went on to show a tooth extraction, the patient groaned and at the end of the procedure the dentist turned to the screen with blood all over his tabard while holding up the extracted tooth and said. "Now look after your teeth!" Well as you can imagine this cured my hiccups!

When my filling was finally done Mr Sucregum gave me a reward sticker? The sticker had a set of smiley teeth on it and the words "I know the Drill!" it was very odd.

After the filling my lips looked very swollen, the receptionist looked at me sympathetically while I paid for the filling.

I then had to do some shopping in Snobihill. You should have seen the looks I was getting. Children were being pulled away from me. My lips were so hideously swollen I looked like a duck.

It wasn't until I got home and the anaesthetic had worn off that I found a huge piece of sponge under my lip. The Dentist had forgotten to take it out!

Friday 27th February

Colder than yesterday!

I realised I had forgotten half the things I was going to buy yesterday so I decided to go into Snobihill again. I was sitting at the Coffee and Drop in Café watching the world go by when who should walk through the door but Marjorie Buttery, who I hadn't seen since we were at Taekwondo classes in the nineties. We had joined Taekwondo as we both thought that the essential rape alarm that always seemed to find its way right to the bottom of your handbag wasn't enough of a deterrent should you be attacked.

Not that Marjorie need of worried she had the appearance of a Rottweiler with lipstick.

She hadn't changed a bit!

Her complexion though had taken on the same colour as my teak cabinet at home.

Marjorie joined me. I then made the mistake of asking

her if she had been away on holiday. I don't think I spoke again for over half an hour. The gist of her story was that she had been to Spain on an all-inclusive holiday for three weeks. She had only gone to see if the warmer climate would stop her post nasal drip. She had though in her words taken with her," her post marital drip of a husband Barry".

Well, on day one they had gone mad as it was all inclusive and drank rather too much Sangria.

One thing led to another and Lord knows how it happened but Barry got quite amorous.

He did something he had never done before, he sucked her big toe. Being "In the moment" and full of Sangria, Marjorie had completely forgotten about her fungal infection. This had been picked up two weeks earlier at the local swimming baths while attending a class with the Cocks Green Ladies Water Aerobics Club.

Marjorie had decided as her toenails were in such a state with the infection to put on false toe nails.

Sadly, Barry was unaware of any of this and got more or perhaps less than he bargained for when the false nail on her big toe came off and choked him.

He spent five days in a Spanish hospital, they managed to extract the false nail but couldn't work out what infection he has picked up. The Doctor said he had never seen a verruca on someone's throat before.

Well, as you can imagine not much of my lemon curd

muffin got eaten after listening to that tale.

I wonder whatever happened to my rape alarm? It's probably still at the bottom of one of my handbags.

Saturday 28th February

It's feels warmer at last it's a barmy fifteen degrees.

Saturdays are always difficult to fill, so I booked Gail to get my nails done and have a chat. She was due at 10.02am. I noticed her van outside at 9am and thought she was early. Then her van disappeared and then returned twenty minutes later.

At 10.20am Gail arrived. "Am Sorry am late, jus bin at the Major's givin im a Back, Crack and Sack. I'd run out of wax before I had even finished the sack, so ad to go home and get some more" explained Gail as she walked in the door.

I felt a bit queasy at the thought.

Gail painted my nails "Pentonville Blue"!

Afterwards she touched up my hair and made me look presentable.

Thankfully later this morning Jane Roid phoned to ask me to go to a games night at the Corn and Callous our local pub.

I jumped straight at the chance and arranged to see her

there at 7.30pm.

It wasn't a great night, I thought I might meet somebody but no such luck.

I started the night playing Monopoly and ended up in jail four times. The very posh serious man opposite who I had seen at the Richard Bow quiz the other night, made a point " Don't you think this game reflects society today, once in prison you're more likely to return and then when you get out the world and friends have progressed and moved on, you find you have very little chance of winning in life!" he proclaimed

"Not really" I replied "How could you possibly win second prize in a beauty competition?"

It was a bit rude of me but he was driving me mad.

Thankfully I was out very quickly after landing on his hotel on Mayfair.

I moved onto Charades, that was better but I wasn't happy when Pete the man in our team ruined my hair by rubbing a balloon against his chest and putting it over my head as I sat in my chair, every curl unravelled itself as my hair reached for the ceiling through the static incurred. "The Green Mile" shouted someone and won!

I ended the night playing Frustration with three old ladies. This summed up the night!

I spent an hour pressing the Popomatic for everyone as neither of the ladies playing had the strength to press it.

Sunday 1ˢᵗ March

Sunny and Crisp. St David's Day.

I walked down to Church this morning with the Major who was wearing a Daffodil. "Are you of Welsh descent?" I asked him. "Bloody Hell Gal! Not a bit. I'm English through and through, although strangely enough I am partial to a spot of Welsh Rarebit" he replied "No harm in giving our Celtic neighbours some support though, after all we have to thank them for giving us Katherine Jenkins!".

Father Aweigh led the service this morning but I must say he made two errors.

Firstly, he stated at the start of the Service, "Would everyone please take a Leak before leaving today". Well I knew what he meant as I saw the Leaks in a basket on the way in but to sow that seed to an elderly congregation meant that at least ten were making their way to the toilet before we had got half way through singing "Bread of Heaven" which was our first hymn.

By the waft in the air later in the service a few didn't quite make it in time!

We have a Welsh couple in our congregation, Mr and Mrs G Evans. I always thought it would be lovely if the G stood for good. But apparently, it's Gareth and Blodwyn.

Father Aweigh though didn't ask either of them to read the prayers today, instead he asked local celebrity Barry

Da who was a well-known Welsh comedian in the seventies. I had never heard of him.

Well it was quite obvious he had never been in a church in his life. His prayers were very strange.

Barry stood at the Lectern and led us in prayer with his very strong Welsh accent. We prayed for the Welsh rugby International Thomas Thomas who had an ongoing injury. We prayed for the Welsh rugby team, we prayed for Barry's Uncle Selwyn's ferret, for the Welsh Assembly, Neil Kinnock, for Barry's Daffodils in his back garden, for Barry itself, not Barry Da but for Barry Island and the customers of Barry Island Working Men's Club.

"Finally", said Barry Da lowering the tone of his voice and sounding very sombre he looked straight at Gareth and Blodwyn "Can we also please pray for our very own Gareth Evans who has been suffering for a long time? Don't worry he isn't ill or anything, it's just that Blodwyn is a nightmare to live with apparently!"

On that note he sat down without so much as an Amen. The congregation were aghast. Except for the Major who let out a loud chortle before trying to turn it into cough.

I did find the expressions on everyone's faces amusing, all avoiding staring in poor Blodwyn's direction.

A very red Father Aweigh quickly went into our last Hymn "Guide me O thy Great Redeemer"

I spent the rest of the day at home, I watched Songs of Praise later and reflected on this morning.

Monday 2nd March

Sunny but cold again.

Drama Day today, that started early when I awoke in a start as "Ted" my newly purchased six-foot Teddy Bear had somehow managed to get right on top of me. I woke up nose to nose with him. It really did make me jump. He may have to go back it is just too big. He takes most of the duvet too. I might as well just get a man!

Today is Drama day so I practiced twerking and singing "I love the smell of Formi-ica" for most of the day.

Emily arrived and we walked down to the Village Hall. Today Everard was dressed like Noel Coward in a paisley silk dressing gown and was holding a long Cigarette holder with a Vaping Cigarette in the end of it? "Greeting my angels" he said in a posher voice than usual, as we walked in through so much vapour smoke it was like being a contestant on "Stars in your eyes".

Later Everard made the two lead roles sing "Tonight". It wasn't until they had sung the revised lyrics, I realised that this play was also about class distinction.

"Tonight tonight, they've stopped their dole tonight"

"Tonight, there will be no Daily Star"

All these weeks I have been coming and didn't realise that the Vests are working class and Shirts upper class. How stupid was I. This farce now had some edge.

Dave Revel Tallwood. DRT as we now call him, then appeared through the vapour cloud and pirouetted into the middle of the hall.

This week we had to practice "Flossing" I got very confused as I thought he meant flossing my teeth.

When DRT showed us how to do it, I was even more confused. Mr Tickle would have made a better job of it.

"Hip action gives me hip action" shouted DRT but it was a lost cause if I had carried on there would have been some displaced hip action!

Something else to practice for next week.

Tuesday 3rd March

Sunny and a little warmer.

A lovely day, it makes so much difference to how you feel. Spring really is in the air. Today I am full of optimism or at least I was until I decided to go to the Library.

I had been asked by Jane if the three Nubile Nymphs would like to attend another Quiz night at our local Pub the Corn and Callous a week Saturday. The questions are about our standard but if we all took a subject each and studied it, it may just give us a better than fighting chance of winning. Jane then asked if I would look at Greek Mythology!

Stupidly I said yes, so now I have to go the Library to get some books on the subject as I know nothing about Greek Myth's.

I haven't been into Snobihill Library since I was a child, it was quite an adventure.

The Librarian took me to the section I required and I spent most of the afternoon reading and selecting the six books required.

It was when I took the books I needed to borrow to the counter to get them date stamped that my day took a turn for the worse.

"I was a member in 1954" I informed the Librarian "Would I still be on your records or will I need a new Library tickets?" I enquired. The very tall lady in a twin set looked down her very large nose through her glasses which were perched on the end of it. "What's the name?" she asked "Now or then?" I replied

She then started looking for a Mrs Noworthen in her records.

I stopped her "In 1954 I was Miss Ophelia Weeklea" I informed her.

She then looked again after tutting!

"Would you be Miss Ophelia Weeklea of 26 Gasbag

Street Snobihill?" asked the Librarian.

Astonished I replied "Yes, that's me"

The Librarian looked at me with distain, "The reason you are still on our records is because you still haven't returned "Enid Blyton's, Five go to Smugglers Top" last seen in this Library in October 1954. Where is it?" she sounded angry.

"How the hell do I know!" I replied

"Well until it's returned there will be no further books loaned to you. Did you not get our letters regarding it being overdue, in fact according to our records one was sent out only last week?" proclaimed the Librarian.

"What! Gasbag Street was turned into an industrial estate in 1979 it doesn't even exist now" I explained.

"That may be the case but there is still the fine to pay!" demanded the Librarian

"Fine what fine?" I enquired

"The fine for an overdue book. Luckily for you this was frozen in 1992 at £378. Do you want to pay for it now by card?" enquired the Librarian.

It was at this point I put the books down on the counter and left in a hurry.

Now I am worried that I will be on CCTV and hounded by the Council for this fine.

Knowing my luck that damn picture of me will be on the front of the Hampton Bugle again!

Wednesday 4ᵗʰ March

A lovely day between the showers.

It's National Salt Awareness week, what on earth does that mean?

A quiet morning, I somehow managed to get the floss stuck between my teeth this morning that wasted an hour trying to get the damn stuff out.

This afternoon it was the U3A meeting. I arrived at the meeting and struggled to get a seat, there was loads of people I had never seen before. The speaker was a Lady called Diana from Ross on Wye.

I am sure a lot of the members thought it was going to be Diana Ross!

Diana was a very smart petite lady dressed in a neatly fitted black dress, black shoes and a silver watch on her wrist, she was about 65 years old.

Her subject was called "The Time of my life" it was about her life and the watch on her wrist.

Well talk about making us all feel inferior. Her list of achievements just went on and on.

She received the watch as a present aged 18 from her

father who had made every cog and spring by hand. He gave the watch to Diana prior to her going to University.

She graduated with honours at Oxford University. She had found a cure for some rare disease in Africa. She had been made a Dame for her Charity work. She had married and divorced a Duke. She had entertained Nelson Mandela at her home.

She had spent three months on the streets living with and helping the homeless.

She had fought for Women's Rights in India. She had recently done a parachute jump to raise money for spectacles for the elderly in Brazil.

Only last week she had given mouth to mouth resuscitation to a Labrador who was a guide dog to a blind old lady. The dog had collapsed in front of her so Diana had applied her veterinary skills she had picked up in Borneo whilst saving the Red Bottomed Chimp from extinction.

All this and her watch had never lost a second, which reminded her every day of the sacrifices her father had made to give her these opportunities.

She then wiped a tear from her eye and told a moving story about her father's last day on earth.

For her Fathers eightieth birthday she had taken him as a special treat to the Worty's Original Toffee factory in Cleethorpes as the factory run a tour once a month.

Worty's Original were his favourite toffee as is the case with most of the elderly. He was thrilled.

He said on that particular morning, that he felt like Charlie in Willie Wonka. Diana stopped at this point to compose herself as her voice became croaky.

"Dad" she said "now needed a walking stick, he would polish that stick with linseed oil every day until it gleamed. He was a very proud man"

She continued "Well during the tour my father rushed to look at the vat of the molten Worty toffee mixture, unfortunately his walking stick somehow managed to get lodged in the grating in front of the bubbling vat and both stick and my father went over the protective railing like an olympic pole vaulter. It was awful."

The whole hall fell silent as Diana once again composed herself.

"It was strange and dreadful at the same time. When my father was finally pulled from the molten toffee, the toffee had coated him completely except for the walking stick which was still in his hand this had no toffee on it at all. It must have been all those layers of linseed oil stopping any adhesion." She poised herself again and then in a whisper said "My father was now dead ladies and gentlemen and had taken on the appearance of a toffee apple" she paused wiped a tear and continued.

"Every day I look at my watch and every day I have a packet of Worty's Originals in my handbag to remind me of my father."

Well everyone looked upset, a few hankies appeared in the audience.

Finally, she told us of her latest venture saving the Nomadic Budgie Tribe and their rare Tiki tiki cows who live in the Brazilian rain forest. The Charity is called "Where ever I lay my "pat" that's my home"

She then looked at us all from the stage and said "What have you done in your life? Have you ever thought about others less fortunate?" We did feel a sense of guilt.

Diana was trying to raise ten thousand pounds for the Tiki tiki cows and could we please give what we could to help.

Money was duly being dropped into the donation box at a great rate. I noticed the Major was amazingly generous and put forty pounds in the box.

Just as his money disappeared into the charity box slot, five men stood up and stormed the stage pinning Diana to the ground.

What a commotion. It was an undercover Police operation, apparently Diana was not all she made herself out to be. The whole thing had been a scam.

The Major was distraught "I've just put fifty pound in that box!" he proclaimed seizing an opportunity to make ten pounds!

But the box was taken away for evidence, Diana was also taken away in handcuffs.

Fortunately, I hadn't got as far as the donation box so my money went back in my pocket.

What a day this turned out to be!

Thursday 5th March

Warm. Daffodils are out everywhere.

I went for a walk this morning as it is a lovely day. Jane Roid joined me, it was only a walk around the local area but living in the countryside means there are plenty of different walks to do.

Emma, Jane's daughter is no longer with Billy Shufflecock as she couldn't risk kissing him, not until one of the them had their braces removed. Jane was pleased about that. "Just as well they have split up, I think Billy was getting to keen, only last week he had written "I love you" in mayonnaise on Emma's cheesy chips!" said Jane

She also said that her Clio's big end was in need of some attention. I don't know why but I thought her sister was named Clio so the conversation went on while we walked with me being very puzzled. When Jane said "Her Clio has had so many things wrong with her lately that she may as well be put on the scrapheap as it's costing a fortune getting her right, her chassis isn't great either."

I thought that was a bit harsh. It was ten minutes in

before I realised, we were talking about her car!

Later that day I watched TV. Not wanting to rant as that's not me at all! But I am sure the world has gone mad.

Four pm in the afternoon the programme I was watching warned me that the programme contained flashing lights and items that viewers may find distressing! When it was over there was a help line number for anyone who had been affected by this programme.

What was the programme? Sooty and Sweep! Sue was depressed because Sooty had squirted water in her face. Sweep had sounded like he was having a fit after a bag of flour had fallen on his head.

He was lying on his back squeaking away as he does, I thought he was laughing!

Sooty had also been subjected to a stop and search by Sue who was trying to find his water pistol!

I do think sometimes we are reading too much into this, I was going to watch Blue Peter but thought better of it. It's a wonder they haven't been asked to change the name in case it upsets a Smurf!

I practiced flossing and twerking in my living room this evening, later I noticed there was a chink in the curtains. I bet the Major has spotted me. Oh dear, I am sure I will know when I next see him.

Friday 6ᵗʰ March

Still Sunny amazing!

Perfect day for gardening today so I manicured my Squirrel Nutkin this morning. It's a topiary clipped hedge in my front garden.

Later I went down to the Knit Wits Club for a bit of Knitting and a chat with the group.

Veronica was very distressed this week! She had been tending to her border in the front garden leaving her antique Ear Trumpet and Zimmer frame on the lawn just behind her.

When she turned around, she noticed that the Ear Trumpet and Zimmer frame had been taken by the scrap man, she saw them both on the back of his lorry as he drove off.

We did manage to get her a replacement Zimmer frame as Jane knew somebody who had one, but the Trumpet was a different matter.

Why she uses it I don't know she has got a pair of hearing aids. Old habits die hard I suppose.

Bernadette O'Leary joined us today, I think she just wanted to chat and let off steam.

She told us about her son Joseph. Her story went as follows I think, as her Irish accent is very strong!

Bernadette had been cleaning the Church when she

noticed her son Joseph enter the Church and go straight into the confessional box. Somehow Bernadette while dusting the pew next to the confessional box had managed to hear what Joseph was confessing!

She couldn't possibly tell us what he had confessed too, but she was appalled at the leniency of the penance given out by Father Aweigh. "Two Hail Mary's, was all he was given. Well I tell you now he got more than that when he come out. I clipped him around the ear as soon as he appeared. I then made him add four Our Fathers and go through the Rosary twice."

"He can also forget going to his friends Stag Night next week as he is grounded for a fortnight" said Bernadette.

"The TV has been taken out of his room too." continued a distraught Bernadette making the sign of the cross and looking to heaven.

Well that got us all thinking. What could he possibly have done?

I did feel sorry for Joseph though as he is twenty-four years old, but nobody argues with Bernadette.

Saturday 7th March

It is pouring down and very windy. What a difference a day makes!

I overslept this morning due to it still being as black as night thanks to the dreadful weather.

Well what a mistake that was, as I had no time to get ready or put hardly any of my make up on before grabbing my paints and rushing down to the Village Hall for the Jan Gough Art Class.

In the short time it had taken me to walk the three hundred yards to the Village Hall my hair had taken on a life of its own and the small amount of mascara I had put on had run down my face.

I was soaked as my brolly had blown inside out as soon as I stepped out of my front door.

I arrived looking awful.

Jan Gough looked at me as I burst through the door, she put her hand to her mouth and whispered "Dear God" to herself.

She then stood up and announced to the group that this week it is "Self Portrait Week!"

To make matters worse she then announced. "These paintings are to be exhibited at the Easter Fete in April, so please do your best work".

Jan asked me if I had bought a photo to work from, I

said I had forgotten. She then took my photo on her Polaroid camera and handed me the result. Well I looked like something from a horror movie if I had been holding a chainsaw over my head with blood dripping from it, I wouldn't have looked out of place!

Jan then announced to the group "You have two hours so please do your best with the photo's you have got with you"

What a nightmare, I did try to ignore the bad hair and make-up, but it was a lost cause.

After an hour my self-portrait looked more like Chi Chi the panda wearing a bird's nest on her head.

I tore that up, and started again. In the end the painting still looked awful I tried to disguise the fact it was me by painting the background vivid blue, red and yellow.

Jan though was very impressed and I was awarded Artist of the Month!

She said "It reflected Edvard Munch and his painting "The Scream" but still retaining an accurate portrait painting of the subject!"

She continued "There is no denying it's you Ophelia"

Jan announced to the group that she would be using my "Masterpiece" on the poster advertising the Art Class at the Easter Fete Art Exhibition.

My heart sank!

Sunday 8th March

Foggy

I went to church this morning, Father Aweigh greeted me as I walked in "Morning Ophelia I think we need a chat sometime this week about the Traffic Calming T. Shirts!" he said.

"What about them?" I said

"I will speak to you later" he said as he greeted Bernadette O'Leary and the other parishioners.

For the whole service he was rabbling on about Genesis, and all I could think about was the T-shirts. Then whilst knocking back the dregs of the communion wine he choked on someone's filling that had been left in the Chalice. Father Aweigh passed out. Nobody owned up to losing a filling, but more to the point I never found out what he was going on about the T-shirt's.

After the Heimlich Manoeuvre had been performed on the Priest by the Major and the kiss of life by a very willing Mrs Beaverbrook, Father Aweigh was in no fit state to talk to anyone when he finally came around.

Mrs Beaverbrook was adamant that resuscitation was five blows into the mouth and one thump on the chest, even though we all disagreed!

When I got home, I thought I would clear out the loft. The old coffee pot is never used that can go to the charity shop but then I remembered buying it with my

Mother so that had to stay. An old painting of Barmouth could go but we used to go there as children. A fishing basket, surely that could go as I have never fished in my life, but it belonged to my Father so that too went back in the loft.

The afternoon started with such enthusiasm and finished with me sitting on the stairs looking at old photos through tears of sadness wondering where the years have gone.

Monday 9th March

The Sun is shining it is a lovely day.

I am 72 years old today!

The postman knocked twice on my door he doesn't always do that!

He had a parcel for me as well as a few cards and a Council tax reminder.

The parcel was from my brother Titan, I opened it to find a book titled "Twerking for the elderly" I did find it funny and it is the thought that counts.

Emily arrived with a bunch of flowers but no card. "I gave you that a month ago" she reminded me.

Emily stayed with me today and we had some lunch. Later we went down to the Drama Group.

Everard met us at the door, today he was wearing a very tight-fitting gold lam'e jump suit, he looked like a giant "Oscar".

Everard seemed more excited that usual if that were possible. "Hurry in girls, everyone is waiting inside for me to reveal my big announcement!" said a very hyper Everard.

Emily replied "Don't worry, in that gold jump suit we have already seen your big announcement!" Everard looked quite shocked.

Everard then leapt onto the stage and began to tell us all about his big announcement.

"As you may have heard our current lead roles have refused to carry on with their roles as Maria and Tony for personal reasons. I have therefore searched high and low for replacement's and I have found two gems in the sand.

Ladies and Gentlemen, I give you Cordelia Pengleton-Smithe and Wayne Bloggs" Everard turned with his arm out pointing to stage left. Cordelia and Wayne came onto the stage from the right!

Cordelia was wearing an Armani camel coat and had a Pug poking his head out of her handbag.

Wayne had his donkey jacket on and was carrying his empty tupperware lunchbox under his arm.

I assumed by the smell that the crab paste sandwiches

once in the lunchbox has just been consumed.

Both took a bow and we applauded.

They then sang a duet from the score of Back Side Story. One Hand, One Heart which of course had now become "One Burp, One Fart". Even so it was beautiful, I had no idea Wayne could sing.

I spoke to Wayne a little later to ask him how he got the role. He explained "I was in the chippy with me other arf Gail. Everard was jus behind me. I sed to Gail "There's a plaice for us" pointin at the last plaice amongst the cod. Everard tapped me on my shoulder and said "Sing it darling, sing it" So I did and ere I am." Said Wayne

"I did perform as Benny in ar school play "Crossroads the Musical" so I'm no novice!" He concluded.

I am not so sure about my new theatrical daughter Cordelia Pengleton -Smythe there's something about that name that rings a bell but can't think why.

A nice birthday though.

Tuesday 10ᵗʰ March

Turned out nice again. Sunny

Our Local Pub, the Corn and Callus is now under new ownership. This is the reason we had the Games Night the other night and this is why we are having a Quiz Night this Saturday. Cyril the owner is changing things for the better, the previous owner was only interested in his Special Brews from around the world.

Lunchtime I arranged to meet Emily in there for a drink and a chat. Emily though was late arriving.

The sun was shining through the pubs doors when suddenly it was eclipsed by a huge body casting a dark shadow across the Pub. I thought this must be Emily but no, the shadow was much larger than that, it was in fact the Major. He walked in very gingerly and looking more bow legged than usual, so much so that he looked like he had been holding a beer barrel between his legs.

"Hello Ophelia, mind if I join you?" enquired the Major "Oh and would you mind if I had that comfy seat your sitting on my arse has just been violated and I need something soft to sit on?" he pleaded.

I felt obliged to move. "What are you drinking?" he then asked as he slumped in my chair with a heavy sigh. I didn't dare tell him I was drinking a "Pornstar Martini" otherwise that would have set him off giving me a torrent of abuse and inuendoes. So I said "I'm fine thank you, unlike you, what has happened?"

The Major beckoned to Cyril for his usual tipple and then proceeded to tell me of his woe's

"You know I have an enlarged Prostate? Well do you remember about two years ago I went to get it checked under the NHS?" I looked at the Major and implied that I didn't remember.

He continued his story "The nurse who examined me had talons for nails, so much so that she had got through three lots of latex gloves prior to sticking her finger up my jacksy, I was sore for days. She also dropped the lube all over the floor and I slipped and nearly broke my back when I got off the bed. I vowed that next time I would go private. Well that "next time" was this morning.

So this morning I went to Poopa Private Hospital in Snobihill and this time I saw a male Doctor.

The trouble was he was portlier than myself, he had hands the size of a tennis racquet and fingers the size of a black pudding. But that wasn't all, once the gloves were on and he started the penetration with his fat finger I swear he said "To infinity and beyond!" as he entered my arse. Naturally I said "I beg your pardon, but the Doctor replied "I said there is definitely nothing wrong" but I know what I heard".

After he had finished the examination the Doctor then tugged at the latex glove struggling to get it off his huge hand and the damn thing finally gave up the battle after being stretched about a yard a flung back whipping my backside.

Bloody Hell that hurt I can tell you, hence the reason for requesting this soft chair" explained the Major.

I looked at the Major in disbelief "To infinity and beyond?" I said

"Yes" said the Major "I know what I heard but how do I prove it?"

Emily then walked in and sat down and immediately said "Morning are you joining us Saturday for the quiz again Major?"

Brilliant another girls night out ruined, Emily said "she just assumed he was coming", well he is now!

Wednesday 11th March

Very windy but sunny.

I had just settled down to watch Lorraine this morning when I heard such a commotion from the back garden.

The Major was obviously still in a bad mood after yesterday's incident. He was having a right go at our resident Dalai Lama Roger Holly who lives between me and the Major at number 4 Ruddy Close.

The Major has never forgiven him for the chicken incident last year.

The Major had put a chicken in his oven and set the timer. The Major had then relaxed in his garden and almost fell asleep. Roger or Buddhist Holly as I call him was sitting in his own garden meditating and chanting as he does most mornings and ended his chant by ringing his newly bought Tibetan Brass Minjira bells.

Unfortunately, the Tibetan Bells had the same ring as the Majors bell on his oven telling the Major that his chicken was cooked and ready to eat.

On hearing the Tibetan Bells the Major thought it was his oven ringing and took the chicken out the oven half an hour earlier than he should have and ate it. He then had gastroenteritis for over a week and ended up in hospital.

This morning Roger had put all his prayer flags on his washing line before starting his morning chant.

The Major looked at the prayer flags and went mad, proclaiming that they were telling the Major were to go in no uncertain terms. He said he could read naval signal flags and Rogers flags were telling the Major to get lost, not quite what the Major said it said, but I couldn't write what he actually said down.

Poor Roger had no idea.

I googled the flags to check and from my side one end did read FFO but that was backwards of course as I was looking from the other side to the Major.

Roger very quickly moved the flags around so as not to

cause offence.

I think his meditation was ruined this morning.

I managed to calm things down but missed Lorraine completely.

I had a phone call later this morning from Wayne informing me that the "Pink One" had had her cholesterol checked and it was through the roof so she has been sent to Hospital for a check-up.

In his words "Ain't no Slimming Club today, Pat Lardy is right mardy and said to tell ya, go with the Fruit Cake this week, she'll weigh yer next week."

I stopped in all day it seemed endless.

Thursday 12th March

Black as night and raining.

A letter arrived this morning with NHS on the envelope, this is never going to be good news!

I opened it with in trepidation and I was right to do so.

The letter was headed "Congratulations you have been chosen!"

Chosen for what I thought, I read on. As part of a new NHS initiative trials, we are now giving patients over seventy years of age the chance to take this wonderful opportunity.

The NHS are offering to give you the "Double Scopey" the letter read.

Well you would have thought I had won the Lottery the way it was written! On Wednesday 1st April at 11.50am would you please report to Hurtglands Hospital for a Colonoscopy and Endoscopy.

With our new high-tech machine, we can now do both procedures at the same time.

Maximising efficiency and minimising your time in the hospital.

"Collene" the new hi-tech machine will enable us to do both procedures in under 30 minutes.

This is not a major procedure!

Should you wish to listen to some music during the procedure please let us know your choice on arrival. Headphones will be provided.

We advise that you are chaperoned on the day of the procedure.

I didn't bother reading any more as the doorbell rang.

Emily arrived later holding a bag of chips! So much for the diet I thought.

I did show her the letter and after five minutes laughing, she did show some sympathy.

"Well I think you should go what have you got to lose?" said Emily.

"I have an idea for your music…" Emily then started singing "What goes up, must come down" and then Emily started laughing again.

""Please release me!" Would be more appropriate" I replied.

I now have this to worry about for the next three weeks.

Oh, to be twenty again nobody had the urge to probe me when I was twenty.

Friday 13th March

It's Sunny! On Friday the 13th it will never last.

The Hampton Bugle appeared through my letterbox this morning and like a fool I read my horoscope or should that be horrorscope!

I found my star sign Pisces. It read. Mars is aligned with Uranus so expect your love life to take an unexpected turn. Be very aware of past foibles when looking at temptation.

Lucky Colour: Elephants Breath. Lucky Number 5629.

What the hell does that mean. Elephants Breath? What sort of colour is that and who has a Lucky Number in the thousands?

What a waste of time.

Mr Tway then phoned to ask me if I had heard about the traffic calming T-shirts.

I had completely forgotten about that, I remember Father Aweigh mentioning it now Mr Tway reminded me.

"No" I replied "Why?" I enquired.   But Mr Tway wouldn't say but asked if we could have a meeting at the Vicarage on Tuesday evening. Intrigued I agreed.

Mr Tway then rang off but before I had chance to take the phone from my ear it rang again nearly deafening me and almost gave me a heart attack.

The very distinctive black country accent hit my eardrums, Wayne!

"Hi Mrs O, yam eard about Lardy, she's in hospital, her arteries are as furry as me cat apparently. I told yer them Belgium Buns were a mistake!"

He continued " Lardy's in ward 13 on the ground floor. It's the ward in-between the morgue and the chapel of rest. The family ave sed not to visit if there is a S in the day, and not after 4pm except on Mondays but then don't go before 3.30pm. Oh an if you can avoid Fridays the'd be grateful and don't get her over excited"

What a shock Pat Lardy can't be above fifty.

Saturday 14th March

Lovely Sunny Day

This evening it was the pub quiz at the Corn and Callus. I arrived in good time for the 7.30 start the Major was already there he had commandeered four seats and beckoned me over.

It was just as well as the place was full.

"Evening Rammy" said the Major "I have already submitted our usual team name, Three Nubile Nymphs and a Nutter ride again" he chuckled.

My heart sank!

Jane and Emily arrived soon after.

Thankfully the team names were less professional than Richard Boes quiz. We had the "Lard Arses" the "Chuckle Sisters" the "Clueless Cooks Clan" the "Universally Challenged" and "Blisters are doing it for themselves" to name but a few, some of the others were very rude.

Cyril the landlord had excelled himself he was wearing a sequin jacket and hosted the quiz, He could hardly contain himself as he read all the team names out.

This was going to be a fun night.

We received our "Picture Round" which was name the hairstyle from the ten pictures provided, that was hard.

The Beehive and Bob were the only two we knew we guessed the rest. Who has ever heard of the classic pompadour and the spikey modern?

The second-round answers had a common theme, some of the answers being, Camp Coffee, Campanology, Mein Kampf, and one we didn't get was "What did Wellington stick up before the battle of Waterloo".

The Major put down "Two fingers to Napoleon"! The answer was of course "Camp"!

We then had a Dance Round, Cyril performed several dances without music and we had to guess what the dance was. Well we didn't do too bad. The Locomotion, Bump, Bunny Hop, Twerking and Flossing were all correct but we struggled with Waacking, Boogaloo, and his Turkey Trot left a lot to be desired. But very funny all the same.

We had a break after that so Cyril could get his breath back.

Then we had the "Make Up" round. Cyril described a make up product from the description on the packaging and we had to guess what it was. The team of Hells Angels in the corner were not happy at all with this round but surprisingly they scored eight out of ten and played their joker giving them sixteen points!

They said it was thanks to "Tripod" who was a member of their team being a big fan of the group "Kiss"

"Kiss my arse" muttered the Major a little too loudly causing everyone to laugh.

After the Hollyoak's Round the final round was the Music Round which consisted of records by Kyle, Madonna, West Life, The Spice Girls, Abba, Vengaboys, Wham and Culture Club.

We ended up finishing fifth overall the Winners being "Gerry and his Pacemaker" but we had a lovely night and I laughed all night long.

Seeing a very drunk Major trying to Floss on the way home was the funniest thing I have seen in ages.

My Tena lady pants had their work cut out I can tell you!

Sunday 15th March

Another Lovely Day

On my way to Church this morning I noticed ahead of me was Wendy Miller and Oscar, I very quickly caught them up not that I was walking fast!

Oscar was wearing one of those funnel things around his neck, what has that poor dog have done now I thought!

"Morning Wendy" I shouted as I approached her.

At this point Oscar jumped and veered towards the privet hedge.

"Please don't shout" said Wendy "your frightening Oscar"

Apart from the funnel, I noticed Oscar had what looked like a hearing aid attachment just behind his ear, the ones that clip to your head.

Wendy explained. "The Vet had noticed that apart from his eyesight Oscars hearing was failing too.

The Vet has fitted Oscar with a Cochlear Implant! The trouble is they have put the funnel on to stop him scratching it. This is just for a few weeks until he gets used to it"

"Is that a problem?" I asked

"Yes" said Wendy "The funnel is acting like an enormous receiver so now poor Oscar is having sound magnified tenfold. "What with that and the hearing aid the dog is petrified every time someone speaks. He is also bumping into everything due to his poor sight and with the funnel his spatial awareness is impaired" Wendy explained

Wendy continued "I am now speaking in whispers, not easy after having years of having to shout, I keep forgetting. Poor Oscar I am sure he will die of a heart attack from the shock"

Just then Jane Roid past in the car and peeped her horn. Oscar took flight and pulled Wendy into someone's garden. I rushed to pick her up and tried to straighten the daffodils she had flattened.

Later there was a terrible incident at Church. Our elderly congregation are dropping like flies. Phil Collins our oldest church member aged 102 years old died ironically while Genesis was being read although I think I was the only one that made the connection!

We all thought he was deep in prayer as he hadn't move for ages.

When it came for time for Communion, he still didn't move, we then realised something was wrong.

After a lovely day yesterday, it is a complete contrast today.

As you get older it feels like everyone you know is leaving the party and you are slowly becoming the only one left. It is not a nice feeling. Twelve funerals last year!

Thankfully not mine!

Monday 16th March

Cloudy.

Not much happening this morning which is just as well as I don't feel great.

This afternoon Emily picked me up and we both went to Hurtglands Hospital to see Pat Lardy. This being in the one-hour slot allowed by the family.

At a push the Hospital would allow four visitors although it should really only be two, in our case seven people had turned up at the same time, all from the Slimming Club. It was chaos!

We tried to pull the curtain around to disguise how many they were of us. Getting around the bed was no mean feat as these are seven large ladies. it very soon became a bit of a free for all.

Then Wayne turned up and shouted across the ward to the nurse "Don't worry I found em, I recognise those three arses even through the curtains, it will be like doin the three peak challenge getting past them". Talk about embarrassing!

Fatima Berg knocked Pats Lardy's drip over, and Pat herself went into a panic attack due to the heat and the claustrophobic situation. We were all getting very hot.

A Nurse then came and told us to leave as Pat was now very distressed. What a waste of time.

Emily stayed at my house this afternoon as we had Drama Group this evening.

As we walked into Drama Group this evening a very excited Everard greeted us both at the door, "Change of plan Ladies, I am going to reveal all in a few minutes!"

A change of attire would have been a better idea. Everard purple shirt and lime green trousers did clash with his yellow braces.

Then somehow as we walked in, he was already on the stage! I am not sure how he does that?

"Now I know I said I had a big announcement last week, but this week it's even bigger!" said Everard

"Due to the Little Hampton WI booking the hall for their naked calendar shoot in June we have now got to move the date of our play "Backside Story" the only week available is the last week in April!"

He looked at us all and pulled a face not unlike Wallace from Wallace and Gromit.

Wayne was the first to respond "Blimey six weeks, it will take me that long to master me Twerking"

But nothing could be done so we now have to knuckle down and do the best we can.

We sang all the songs from the play this evening and it wasn't great. My song "I love the smell of Formi-ica" was ok if a little pitchy.

Emily enjoyed being surrounded by all the boys as they sang "Gee Officer Krapknee" and fortunately she doesn't have to sing!

Wayne's rendition of "Somethings Coming" now called "Somethings Humming" while sniffing his armpits was applauded by Everard who thought it was brilliant!

Tuesday 17th March

Gloomy. St Patricks day.

For some reason I felt the urge to go to Church this morning, there was a short service due to it being St Patricks Day.

Only a few of us attended, Bernadette O'Leary, Mrs Beaverbrook, Mr Crabtree and a couple of others.

Afterwards I had a cup of tea and made the mistake of talking to Mr Crabtree.

Mr Crabtree and his wife Ethel live in Whet Bottom a village a few miles away. Both are in their late eighties.

Ethel though was noticeable by her absence. As I thought she may be dead and nobody had told me I tentatively asked him how she was.

Before I relay this weird conversation, I have to say that Mr Crabtree gets very mixed up and if you correct him, he always says "That's what I said"

When replying to my enquiry about Mrs Crabtree he replied.

"Oh, I'm glad you asked" said Mr Crabtree in his Lancashire accent "She has gone to Ibiza for a fortnight. She's having the time of her month with her eldest sister Maud."

I assumed he meant "Time of her life" but I didn't say anything.

"Yes" he continued "She said, she is trying to tick off all the things she wants to do off her shopping list before she pegs out her washing and dies"

"Bucket List" I said under my breath.

"The next thing she said she wants to do is swim with donkeys, God knows why!" he said shrugging his shoulders.

"Dolphin's" I thought getting quite frustrated

"Only last Month she dropped from a great height hanging from a wire by her zip!". He continued

"Anyway, it will be the death of her all this business if she's not careful, she has already been ill eating that Salmonella Pudding or some out" said Mr Crabtree and continued

"She been trying to get me to use that "Face Crime" so I can speak to her face, but I've no idea about that sort of stuff, so now she keeps contacting me by text and ending her texts with that hash brown nonsense. Hash brown sunset. Hash brown bare feet. I've not a clue what it all means.

I finally had to intervene and said "You mean Hashtag" to which he replied "That's what I said!"

Father Aweigh then appeared thank goodness to remind me that I would see him later for the Humping Meeting with Mr Tway.

I went home feeling very tense, and had to have a lie

down. Emily phoned to say she would go straight to Father Aweighs this evening, but she wanted to know if I wanted tickets for the "Mystery Tour" Coach trip tomorrow as there are two cancelled seats going free. I said I would go. Anything to lift my spirits!

Things didn't improve this evening at the humping meeting.

I arrived at Father Aweighs house. Mr Tway and Emily were already there.

Mr Tway looked very worried. Next to him was a large cardboard box.

He then spoke "I called this meeting to discuss the Humping T-shirt's we agreed to have made and printed."

We all nodded

"That's right" I said "If I remember rightly we were having numerous sizes with "No Traffic Calming Please on my Little Hampton" printed on the front. I think we asked you to ordered fifty?" I enquired.

Mr Tway replied "That's right" the supplier said he would only give a discount on price if we ordered a hundred and we reduced the lettering as "No Traffic Calming Please on my Little Hampton" was more than a T-shirt could cope with. If you wanted to make a bold statement the lettering would be too small you see"

Mr Tway continued "So I said he knew best and I would leave it with him"

We all looked at each other puzzled.

Mr Tway then pulled a T-shirt from the box.

Well I managed to contain myself as we were in the company of Father Aweigh, Emily though did not, which was a little embarrassing when she said "What the bloody hell is that" I was relieved it was only the word "bloody" she had used.

Mr Tway held up one of the one hundred T-shirt's for us all to see.

It read "No TCP on my Little Hampton"

What a load of idiots we are going to look wearing those.

But nothing can be done as Mr Tway had already paid for them.

This Campaign is not going well.

 # Crapday   # Madhouse

Wednesday 18th March

Raining

This morning there was an air of anticipation in spite of the weather.

The mystery coach trip this morning is leaving Snobihill at 9.30am, I only hope that it is going to take us to sunnier climes.

Emily picked me up at 8.30am and we got to Snobihill in good time, the coach was waiting as we arrived. "Mystery Tour" read the destination sign on the front of the coach.

It was quite exciting.

Once everybody was on the coach the driver Gary made an announcement.

"Morning Campers, just a few announcements before we set off to Rhyl." Said Gary.

You could hear the groans all around from the passengers, "Thanks for ruining the mystery" shouted an elderly man from the back of the coach.

Gary started laughing "Calm down everybody that was my little joke we are not going to Rhyl. I do have to make these announcements though.

There will not be a toilet stop on this journey but so as to not spoil your enjoyment we have provided incontinence pads which you will find in the pouch on the back of the seat in front of you.

Should you need to use them there is a plastic bag provided to deposit the pad into.

At the end of the journey my assistant Sharon will collect them from you when we reach our "Mystery" destination!" he concluded.

I nervously looked around me, all the passengers had a look of horror and panic on their faces.

Gary then burst into laughter "Got you all again, I'm only joking!"

Gary continued. "Right if we are all ready? As PJ and Duncan said "Let's get ready to rumble" "shouted Gary. The aforementioned song then blasted out of every speaker in the coach.

Well that sent all the hearing aids whistling I can tell you.

With that he started the engine.

Two hundred yards down the road his Sat Nav said. "Turn around when possible!"

I heard a very worried old lady in front of say "I do hope they have told the driver where we are going, I would hate to get lost!"

Three miles into the journey, Gary got our hopes up of a seaside destination by playing Cliff Richard singing "Summer Holiday". He then encouraged us all to join in, which we did.

Then a bizarre thing happened Gary stopped the coach as a man was at the side of the road thumbing a lift.

"Do you want a lift?" Gary asked the hitchhiker.

"Where yer going" asked the hitchhiker.

"I can't tell you that it's a closely guarded secret. It's a mystery tour" replied Gary.

"I'll take me chances" said the hitchhiker and got on the coach?

He sat down next to Sharon and off we went.

Gary was now driving on the M6 going north when he announced with a chuckle, "Don't worry about food there's a "top notch café" where we are going!"

He continued "There will also be a strapping lad there too!"

"The clues are there everyone, does anyone have any idea where we are going?" asked Gary

Nobody had a clue. But the nervous old lady in front looked very worried and screamed "Oh my God, he doesn't know where we are going, we are lost"

I had to calm her down.

Thankfully thirty-five minutes later we stopped.

"Right" said Gary "I hope you enjoy your day, if you could all be back on the coach by 3.30pm on the dot. Don't forget my saying "If you delay you stay" in other words I leave at 3.30pm whatever and no excuses accepted if your late, I've heard them all. You have been warned!"

We had arrived at "The Leather Museum" in Walsall. Well, nothing against the Museum but when you are expecting a trip to London or day in Bournemouth it was a disappointment.

Most of the passengers had been to the Museum before.

The average time spent visiting the Museum was one hour and eighteen minutes, we were not due back on the Coach for five hours!

The group all went to the Museum and afterwards had lunch in a local pub "The Ailing Sadler".

It was in the Pub I hit upon an idea to get one over that arrogant coach driver Gary.

Myself and Emily went around the group suggesting that as we were all pensioners, we could all use our free bus and train passes and be home by 2pm.

So that's what we did, but not a word was said to Gary or Sharon.

Lord only knows what happened at 3.30pm when nobody returned to his coach, he is probably still there now asking if anyone has seen forty-two pensioners, serves him right.

Thursday 19th March

Sunny and it's National Poultry Day!

I assume someone has told the chickens, I would hate them to miss out!

Being National Poultry day, reminded me that I needed some provisions so I went down to the Two Stop Shop in our village.

Mr Khan was having another altercation, this time it was with Mrs Beaverbrook.

Mrs Beaverbrook was not happy and was banging a french stick on the counter in time with every word spoken.

"First we had the rude words in the spaghetti that Mrs O'Leary had to endure and now this with the bread." Shouted Mrs Beaverbrook.

I was intrigued

"How in God's name does a slice of toast get into a loaf of bread when it has never been opened?" enquired Mrs Beaverbrook.

"Mr Khan shrugged his shoulders "I don't know, it is the third incident this week. I have asked the bakery to check. But they said it is not their end it is impossible with the stringent hygiene policy they have."

"You know you should change the shop name to "Utter Khanage" because that's what it has become, you never know what surprise awaits you, I will probably find an egg inside my frozen chicken." Said Mrs BeaverBrook as she slammed the money on the counter and stormed out the shop.

Mr Khan did not look happy.

I tried to make light of it "It could be the next best thing since sliced bread. Ready-made toast!"

"It is not funny, Mrs Ramsbottom. I am becoming a laughing stock. Who would do such a thing?" said Mr Khan?

"What has become of the world? He asked and continued

"My friend heard the ice cream man come around the other day. The Ice Cream Van was called "Smack, Crack and Pop" the jingle he was playing, so I am told was "Lucy in the Sky with Diamonds".

Well my friend got more than he bargained for, the whole family were high on drugs for two days and all they had was a ninety-nine and two cornets. The drugs were in the sprinkles apparently.

He did find it strange that the queue was ten deep at the van!

It is a sad world Mrs Ramsbottom a sad world." Said Mr Khan shaking his head.

I was going to buy a tub of hundred and thousands for my trifle but thought better of it!

I just bought a newspaper instead and left.

A quiet afternoon this afternoon. Emily phoned to ask if I wanted to go and see a Roberta Flack and Desmond Decker tribute group called Flack and Decker workmates.

They are on at Snobihill Theatre in April.

Before saying yes, I did You Tube them, her rendition of "Killing me Softly" would have been better if her teeth hadn't whistled on each word beginning with S. His version of the "Israelites" was ok.

So I have agreed to go.

Friday 20th March

Dark as night, heavy rain.

Emily phoned this morning very upset her boyfriend "Marcel Marcel" who she had met at the Valentine date night, had finished their relationship.

Emily explained "He even finished our relationship in mime, it took me half an hour to work out what he was trying to tell me."

First, he pointed at himself and then Emily, then he shook his head and mimed "No" with his hands.

Emily though thought he was doing his Spice Girls mime of them singing "Stop right now thank you very much"

Then he pretended to walk down some steps waving as he went!

Eventually he mimed being hung by a rope and pointed at himself and Emily.

Putting all this together, Emily somehow made sense of it all and started to cry.

He also mimed crying and produced a bunch of flowers from his sleeve which he gave to her.

"He then left." reflected Emily.

I really didn't know what to say. It is very sad.

Emily is coming around for coffee tomorrow.

The Knit Wits meet this afternoon, I have knitted forty daffodils so hopefully Jane Roid will be pleased.

I arrived at Knit Wits only to find Mrs Catterack in tears. What a day!

Mrs Catterack had agreed to have her gas and electric meter changed to one of the "smart meters" as her bills have always been high.

When I asked how high she said one hundred and fifty pound a month!

She lives on her own it's unbelievable.

The man arrived and changed the meter. He couldn't work out though why the meter was still whizzing round even though he had turned everything off.

He then traced all the electric wiring and to his surprise he realised that Mr Catterack meter is connected to the traffic lights outside her house.

The Electricity man has done a rough estimate and thinks Mr Catterack is paying about £40 a month for the traffic lights. He is still not sure what to do though, he can't disconnect the traffic lights as that would leave the motorists unsafe.

 He has contacted the Council who have contacted the Highways Agency.

Nobody seems to want to take responsibility.

Mrs Catterack is so worried.

"When or how do you think this happened" I asked her.

She seems to recall that her electric meter was put in the same time the Electricity Board dug up the road outside her house to put the new traffic lights in. She had had trouble with her meter which had been flooded so they fitted a new one.

 "Well those Lights have been in years. In fact, I don't think I can remember them not being there" I said.

"I know" said Mrs Catterack "This was in 1977, I remember because it was the Silver Jubilee and I had to move the TV as I could see the reflection of the traffic lights on the Duke of Edinburgh's head on the tv screen.

I thought the cost had gone up because of the new meter they had put in. I didn't say anything in case I owed the Electricity Board some money due to the old meter being faulty."

"You must be owed a fortune. Get onto the Hampton Bugle straight away" I said to her

Mrs Catterack just wanted an easy life and seemed reluctant to do so.

"Right" I said "that's another injustice to be put right!

Saturday 21st March

Sunny today all day.

Still annoyed about Mrs Catterack's traffic light situation, I reckon she has paid twenty thousand pounds for the lights over the past forty years.

She has had to put up with her front living room and bedroom being like a discotech with her rooms changing colour from red to amber and then green. Such is the close proximity of the lights to her house.

She never got any compensation for that either!

I phoned Mrs Catterack this morning, she was really worried now. She said "She didn't want to cause any trouble".

I assure her that I would do what I can and would speak to the Highways Agency and Council first thing Monday.

I have to tread carefully with this as I don't want Mrs Catterack dropping down dead with the worry.

I went down to the Two Stop Shop this morning as I needed some milk.

As soon as I walked in Mr Khan asked me if I remember that protest song by Bob Dylan?

He then started singing "The lights, they are a changing".

"I hear you are seeing red, Ophelia but not as many times as Mrs Catterack eh" He said laughing.

Honestly can nothing be kept quiet in this Village.

Just then the Major walked in. "Morning Rammy, I hear your taking up the mantle with this traffic light situation. Well you may have more on your plate than you thought.

Mr Jones thinks his bills went up when the balisha beacons were changed on the zebra crossing outside his house. Also Wendy Miller now thinks she if paying for the "frail person" crossing sign that is lit up outside her house. "said the Major "All nonsense of course but the whole Village is worried, everyone who has a lamp post outside their house thinks they are paying for it" he said. "The bloody worlds gone mad, Rammy, mad!" The

Major picked up his Telegraph put the money on the counter and walked out.

Why does this always fall on me, on the way home someone held their fist up like a civil rights campaigner to me. One shouted "Keep up the fight Ophelia" and another said "You show them" as they walked past me.

I was glad to get back in the house.

I ignored the phone which must have rang twenty times.

How did this happen?

Emily arrived later she was still in the doldrums after being dumped.

But she cheered up and laughed her head off when I told her of my woes and the traffic light debacle.

So glad she finds it so amusing, it's the last time I show her any sympathy!

Sunday 22nd March

Another lovely sunny day. National Cleaning Week! I must tell Emily!

I went to Church again this morning twice in a week, not done that for a while.

Thankfully, Mr Crabtree was deep in conversation with Mrs Beaverbrook, so I sat in a pew well away from him.

I sat quietly contemplating and closed my eyes as if praying as I was enjoying the time alone.

Fortunately, this seemed to work and nobody disturbed me. With my eyes closed listening to distant echoes of people conversations and the relaxing environment I would have thought I could have got close to God and reflected on my life.

Sadly, my conversation with the man upstairs was interrupted by me thinking that I need bread and milk and worrying if I left the kitchen tap running!

I find it so difficult to switch off.

I tried again and this time it seemed to work, unfortunately though I fell asleep!

It was so embarrassing as I was asleep for ages and started snoring quite loudly right in the middle of Father Aweigh's sermon.

The Major gave me a nudge, I awoke with a start as I had no idea he was sitting next to me.

"I say Ophelia were you asleep or just making a point about how boring this is?" said the Major with a chuckle.

I quickly sat upright and took my head off his shoulder, how that got there I will never know!

At the end of the service Father Aweigh asked if anybody was willing to volunteer?

As I wasn't sure what he was talking so I put my hand up to ask.

Father aweigh looked at me and said "Thank you Ophelia I knew we could depend on you!"

So now I have volunteered myself and I have no idea for what.

I didn't like to say I was only enquiring. The Major was no help either he had no idea what I have put myself up for.

He did however find it very funny.

I stayed in the rest of the day, pottered around the garden and relaxed without being disturbed!

Monday 23rd March

Raining all day

Most of the day was spent on the phone trying to sort out Mrs Catterack's electricity bill.

Mrs Catterack was my first call. She was a bundle of nerves worrying that she may be in trouble. It took me twenty minutes convincing her that she was the victim in this ridiculous situation.

Then I phoned the Council. It had only rang once when an automated message was heard.

"If you have any information regarding the desecration of our staff toilets please press 7 on your keypad now, where a member of our team will discuss this with you." Stated the message.

"Desecration?" That a bit steep I thought., and they now have a designated team working on it!

Then I was diverted to another message as I didn't press 7. "If you are calling about rent arrears, or potholes, press 1. If you are calling about a death in your family, or graffiti, press 2. If you are calling about a Council tax payment, or need counselling yourself, press 3. For anything else press 4."

It all seemed a bit disjointed to me but I pressed 4 and held on for fifteen minutes! Then the phone went dead?

I ended up phoning my friend Lottie as she works there. Lottie directed me to the right number but the lady said it was not a Council matter and I need to speak to the Highways Agency.

I rang the Highways Agency and was put on hold surprisingly. I am sure someone was having a laugh the "hold" music was "What's another year" by Johnny Logan "The opening lyric being "I've been waiting such a long time, looking out for you, but you're not here, what's another year"

Well that rang true after hearing it for the fifth time, then the music changed to "Hanging on the telephone" by Blondie!

Eventually the man I spoke to said "It was a matter for the Electric Company".

I rang the Hampton Bugle as I was getting nowhere and they said they would look into it.

By this time, it was well into the afternoon and I still had to practice flossing before going to Am Dram this evening.

I was exhausted when Emily arrived.

Later we walked to the Village Hall where both Everard and DRT greeted us dressed in black suits?

We both wondered why but didn't ask.

Everard and DRT stood on the stage and explained their attire. "The Matrix Darlings! Think slow mo" explained DRT

We were still none the wiser.

Everard and DRT then started moving towards each other in slow motion, Everard was holding a cucumber and attempted to thrust it at DRT. DRT dodged it while making a beautiful dance move. All in slow motion. They then took a bow and we applauded.

"Now my Angels it's your turn. This is the fight scene between the Vests and the Shirts. This is where Wayne playing Tony stabs Bernard who plays Bernardo" said DRT

Everard handed Bernard his cucumber. "Remember all the action is in slow mo." Said Everard

Well to say it needed some work was an understatement. Bernard was supposed to wrestle with the knife (cucumber) but lost his footing and the cucumber seemed to disappear somewhere as Bernard fell awkwardly on top of Wayne.

We all rushed to Bernard who had Wayne pinned beneath him.

"Bloody ell, yam cud of killed me if that had bin a knife, ya Nutter" shouted Wayne wiping the squashed cucumber off the his crotch.

Fortunately, we all laughed and it diffused the situation.

With only four more rehearsals before opening night I fear it is going to be a disaster.

Tuesday 24th March

The sky grey and it's raining.

I had a phone call this morning from Fatima Berg to say that Pat Lardy had taken a turn for the worse and the outlook was not good.

She then said under no circumstances should we visit, that was a request by the family and the Matron on ward 13.

Fatima is suspending the Cake Diet Club until further notice as a mark of respect.

I was very shocked by this news, I can't say I liked the woman but it was such bad news.

That put a downer on the day.

Emily came over later to play scrabble but neither of us had the appetite for it.

The same went for my lemon drizzle that we had with a cup of tea. Neither of us touched it, I am not sure if it was due to the bad news we had received regarding Pat or the fact we both knew it should really be chelsea bun week, had the Slimming Club been on.

I reminded Emily that it was National Cleaning Week this week, I can't write down her reply.

Emily then said the most bizarre thing. "Guess which

celebrity I stood next to at the cheese counter in Waitloads?" she looked at me with expectation that I would just pull a name out of thin air"

I appeased her by saying "Male or Female?" "Male" came the reply.

I won't go through every question I asked, as that would be a waste of five sheets of paper!

After twenty minutes I narrowed it down to astronomy but in spite of going through every person I could think of I gave up.

Emily looked very keen to tell me and then announced it was Patrick Moore off the TV the presenter of The Sky at Night.

"Don't be stupid" I said rather annoyed having wasted twenty-five minutes of my life. "He has been dead for years!"

Emily said "It must be him he had a monocle and he gave me his autograph".

"It can't be" and thrust my phone under her nose which stated he was no longer on the planet.

Emily looked at his picture but still insisted that it was Patrick Moore. It's unbelievable!

She then left in a bit of a huff.

Wednesday 25ᵗʰ March

Very damp but drying up later.

As there is no Slimming Club today, I decided to go crazy and paint the downstairs toilet.

I went online to look at the paints at P & Q. I was astonished to find that Clown Paint had a new range of paints called "The Human Range". It is a world gone mad.

All I wanted was some green and lemon paint but I was definitely not buying a paint called "Mucus".

Having gone through every green in the range from "Earwax" to "Pus".

I decided on "Discharge" as its green had an ochre tinge to it which complemented the "Bile" yellow paint I wanted for the back wall behind the toilet.

The toilet needed doing thanks mainly to Emily. Lord only knows what she does in there but the walls have a taken on a yellow glow even though it was painted white.

Now I had the job of going to P & Q and buying the paint!

I arrived only to find that the paint was not on display so I had to ask for it.

I felt so stupid asking the P & Q employee where I could find "Discharge" and "Bile" he looked puzzled but eventually pointed to aisle nine.

As I walked away toward aisle nine the assistant shouted "Your "Discharge" is on the third shelf next to a large amount of "Phlegm" and you will find your "Bile" is sitting on top of a load of "Pus" on the next shelf."

I wanted to die!

Sadly the "Bile" paint was nowhere to be seen so they had to make up the paint.

The shaker machine that mixes the paint was broken so I then I had to wait an age for Steven who was the only member of staff qualified to shake the paint.

Shaking Steven then shook my "Bile" for a full three minutes. He looked very red at the end of the ordeal. But the paint had taken on the colour I expected.

A further commotion was then endured trying to pay for the paint as a man was arguing with several assistants, it was the Major. I couldn't see him as he was surrounded by four members of the P & Q staff, his voice though I would recognise anyway.

"But I only want to buy one nail" proclaimed the Major "I do not need a bag of fifty just to hang my coat up!"

At that point I thought it was going to get nasty when a huge P & Q employee advanced on the party arguing. He must have been six foot eight inches at least.

"Right" the huge man shouted "Who wants decking?"

"There's no need to resort to that sort of aggression" said the Major.

The giant ignored him and shouted even louder "Who wants decking?"

A little man then poked his head around from behind the fixtures and said "Me"

"Right" said the orange giant "Is it for a patio in your garden and if so what sort of decking do you need?"

I think we all breathed a sigh of relief.

In the end the manager gave the Major one nail just to get rid of him.

What a day!

Thursday 26th March

Sunny and warmish.

I walked down to the Two Stop Shop this morning and noticed a crowd had gathered outside the shop. "A sad day today Pat Lardy has passed on" Mrs Catterack informed me "She wasn't that old either" she continued.

This was a terrible shock. Just then Wayne arrived to buy his newspaper and cigarettes,

"Wa yer all lookin so glum about?" he enquired. We informed him about the bad news.

"To many bloody cakes that's the trouble, I'm worried about what damaged she's done to me own elth with that bleeding cake diet" he said while smoking his cigarette and eating a large pasty.

"I dunno about passed on, she should have passed on a few of those chelsea buns at Dreggs bakery. If she had she might still be ere!" he proclaimed.

You could see the shock on the ladies faces standing outside the shop.

"Oh, and can any of yow tell Mrs Tushingham if ya see er, that ar Gail can't do er Brazilian tommora so she will pencil her in next Wednesday. Tushy's phone ain working or sumet" said Wayne.

Thankfully he then went into the shop.

This afternoon I started painting the downstairs toilet. How hard can this be.

I am sure this was easier when I last did it, although that was at least ten years ago.

I was about two stone lighter then too!

The problem is the confined space you have to work in. No matter what angles I put my body into getting the brush to go just where I wanted it to go was no mean feat.

After an hour I had managed to get the paint all over the toilet seat. The "Bile" paint then seemed to find its way all over my backside, every time I turned to put my brush in the paint my posterior rubbed against the wall.

In the end I gave up, after a further hour cleaning all the paint off the toilet.

The fumes then made me dizzy and I was overcome with emulsion!

Stupidly without thinking I then sat down in the lounge and got paint all over the seat cushions.

Later I searched through the Yellow pages for a decorator. I phoned "Matt Gloss the decorator" (That can't be his real name surely?) who is coming around next week.

What a rubbish day!

Friday 27th March

Sunny again

Emily contacted me this morning and said there was a clairvoyant in Snobihill town centre called Madam Penipuan the Medium.

Emily was desperate to know if "Joe" her deceased cocker spaniel could be contacted.

"Joe" had been run over by a milk float about two years ago. The float was only going fifteen miles an hour. Not really sure how that happened, talk about slow re-actions by both the dog and the Milkman!

Emily wanted to know if I would go with her this afternoon, once again I reluctantly said "Yes".

We arrived at Madams door where a man was sitting in the booth. "£20 for the full experience. Your future is told and you get to contact a loved one that has passed" said the man.

We paid the £20 each as we entered a dimly light room, there was about ten people sitting. We sat down on the end of the fifth row.

Madam Penipuan then arrived from the back of the room and made her way to the front where her large black armchair faced us awaiting her presence.

Sadly, she tripped over the leg of my chair and went down face first on the floor. She got up quickly and sat down.

"She didn't see that coming!" I whispered to Emily.

Madam then went into a trance started moaning and thrashing her body from side to side, she then shouted "Peter, does the name Peter mean anything to anybody"

"Yes, he's my brother" I replied

"Well he says he is ok and not to worry" said Madam Penipuan

"That's good it will save me texting him later!" I replied.

"Hasn't he passed on?" said Madam Penipuan

"I hope not!" I replied. I must say it worried me a little so I did text him with the message "Are you alive? "He replied "No" so I knew he was ok.

Madam then said "I'm getting a "Joe" coming through does anyone know a "Joe"?"

Emily was getting very excited thinking contact had been made with her dead dog.

Emily stood up and said "Yes that will be my Joe"

Madam continued "He said "I'm getting by with a little help from my friends""

I noticed tears came to Emily's eyes. "That's good" she whispered

I think I ruined the moment by me saying that's the singer Joe Cocker that is, that's his lyrics, not Joe the cocker spaniel!

I couldn't take it seriously.

Half an hour later after ten other random names had been called out to the misguided audience both Emily and I had our palms read by Madam, that was another waste of time.

Emily is going to have a long life, and she was ready to move on to a new level?

I though was a different matter. Madam struggled to find my life line and didn't see anyone new coming into my life.

She then said "Does the number two mean anything to you?"

"I live at number two?" I replied

"Well I see you struggling with number twos for many years to come!" said Madam Penipuan.

I looked her straight in the eyes and said "I have been struggling with number twos for years. It's called constipation!" I then left what a waste of time.

When I got home, I looked up Madam Penipuan the Medium to see if she was at large. I couldn't find her name on the internet at all, but interestingly "Penipuan" is the word for "Fraud" in Indonesian. That speaks volumes!

Saturday 28th March

Pouring down

National Respect your Cat Day!?

The Hampton Bugle appeared through my letter box this morning two days late. This being on account of Mr Tussock delivering them, he is nearly ninety and has a zimmer frame.

I was expecting the headline to be about Mrs Catterack's traffic lights situation but no.

The headline read "TCP banned from Little Hampton" I

read on "T Shirt fiasco" and then "Residents still "smarting" from printing error"

Think or any pun to do with TCP and it was in the report

Apparently, I was "Down in the mouthwash" about the whole thing and that dreadful picture of me was used yet again.

I suppose any publicity is better than none at all, but thanks to Mr Tway's error the group have become a laughing stock.

Mrs Catterack's Traffic Lights ordeal had been relegated to page three.

It was under the headline "Residents see Red, and Amber and Green" followed by "Thousands of pounds owed to locals. All the road sign lighting is being paid for by residents directly allegedly".

This gave me an idea of how to kill two birds with one stone!

We will form a human chain across the road, blocking it in protest of both Mrs Catterack's traffic lights and the "traffic calming prevention".

With so many Residents upset and thinking that every street light is being run off their electric meter, the support could be immense.

I need to call an urgent emergency meeting next week as I have to arrange this before the traffic lights are sorted.

Tomorrow, I will start my campaign, when I go to church and see if I can get them all on board.

After all the top man himself said "Let there be light and there was light" not "Let there be light providing it's run off your meter!"

I am now quite excited, this humiliating day could turn into a positive outcome after all.

Sunday 29ᵗʰ March

Raining

I couldn't sleep last night, probably because of this "human chain" I am trying to organise.

But I am optimistic that we can get the Village together on this.

I went to church this morning hoping that at least a few may be interested.

Father Aweigh greeted me on arrival, "Morning Ophelia, I see your T-shirt's have hit the headlines" he said with a smile.

Once inside and the service started, Father Aweigh asked if anyone had any news?

I walked straight to the front and explained to the congregation what had happened regarding the road humping and Mrs Catterack's Traffic Lights electricity debacle and finally what I intended to do about it.

I found myself hitting the lectern on every word spoken I was enraged. I ended my speech requesting my audience to raise hands if they were behind me.

I don't know what came over me, the whole experience was very empowering.

To my surprise almost everyone put their hands up.

Father Aweigh did give me a ticking off afterwards for using the church to express my views, which I found a bit hypocritical! "You have been doing that for years!" I replied

The response afterwards was fantastic everyone patting me on the back and asking when the human road block will take place?

I also sold seven TCP t-shirts, which was amazing.

I think it is the Traffic Lights that everyone is most annoyed about and several parishioners think they may also be paying for they street lights too!

I then had the misfortune of bumping into old Mr Crabtree!

"Aye up chuck, great speech" he said "So can you just remind me again why have you got the hump just because the traffic lights are changing?"

He obviously had not listened to a word I had said.

"How is Mrs Crabtree?" I enquired changing the subject. That was a mistake!

"Well I dare say you've heard?" said Mr Crabtree.

"Heard what?" I enquired

"About her mishap, jumping with a budgie with an elastic band" he proclaimed

"No?" I replied, thinking what is he going on about.

"Aye Mrs Crabtree, or should I say Ethel and a budgie jumped from a tower holding on to an elastic band, they both plummeted to the ground, fortunately the elastic band broke her fall, but she did take all the skin off the end of her nose as she skimmed the ground" explained Mr Crabtree "It really shook her up, I assume the budgie was a bit shaken too, but she didn't say" explained Mr Crabtree

This took a while to work out, but then it clicked "Bungie jumping!" I said.

"Aye that's what I said" he then went on "Anyway no sooner she's home from Ibiza and she's off again this morning to some place by Costa somewhere near some black Country. She's doing some Hot Yogurt Classes or some out.

"Costa Rica?" I asked

"Nah nearer than that" exclaimed Mr Crabtree looking at me, as if I had gone mad!

"Costa Del Sol?" I asked again. I was getting a bit fed up by this point.

"Nah Costa in Dudley. Yah know that coffee shop place in the Black Country?" Stated Mr Crabtree

I quickly made my excuse and left at this point before going insane.

Monday 30th March

Thunder storms

Woke up in a sweat this morning after a nightmare about that damned "Double Scopey" on Wednesday.

Why I didn't just phone and say "No thank you!" I don't know.

Emily phoned this morning to remind me that it was a full rehearsal this evening for "Back Side Story"

She has asked if she can come around early to practice her lines before going down to the Village Hall later.

I wouldn't mind but all her part consists of is blowing her whistle and shouting "Stop!"

Later on it dawned on me that I haven't thought of an "April fool" to play on the Major this year.

Last year I arranged for Pat our postman to deliver a letter to the Major from the National Thrust which I had typed. The letter informed him that he had won a car in their prize draw and to phone the car dealer to arrange delivery.

The telephone number was a car dealer in Sunderland, as I know the Major always struggles understanding the geordie accent. I could hear him on the phone getting more and more frustrated as he had his kitchen window open. He was an age trying to get to the bottom of what had happened. It was so funny.

This afternoon my heart went up in my mouth, there was a loud bang on the front door. I saw a Policeman at the door.

"Open Up" the Policeman shouted.

I opened the door and there stood Emily dressed as Officer Krapknee, the fool!

Later Emily practiced aggressive whistle blowing for an hour. Lord knows what the neighbours thought.

Then we tried to master Flossing and Twerking, not at the same time I might add.
I sang "I love the smell of formica"

I then put my dress on for A Knitters part. The petticoat had forty-one layers of netting under the dress, so much so I couldn't see where I was going.

It was like sitting on the top of a dandelion!

We headed off to the Village Hall. This was done in single file as there was no way the dress would allow two abreast.

Everard met us at the door dressed in a blue satin onesie. He looked like Andy Pandy.

He took one look at Emily in her uniform. "Officer Krapknee you look fantastico!" he proclaimed kissing the end of his fingers.
He then turned to me "My God! That dress! You look like your knickers have exploded?" he said

"How can you possibly floss in that" he enquired

"Ask Connie our dressmaker to tone it down, I haven't seen a petticoat that big since I watched an episode of "Come Dancing" in 1964!"

The night went well otherwise, the only problem was Everard trying to understand Wayne's accent. "Darling your fine singing but what does "Yam Vests ar gonna av there way tunit ah nay" mean?" he said.

But we all assured Everard that is was much the funnier for it.

Tuesday 31st March

Sunny and warm

Well where did that month go?

I am sure time gets faster and faster, I can't believe three months have gone by.

I received a call today from Lottie Thatcher, the defecator at the Council had been caught red or should that be brown handed.

Anyway, she couldn't reveal the perpetrators name and that was as much as she could say, she was just relieved that the ordeal was over.

No sooner had I put the phone down and it rang again.

This time Emily who was in a right state. "Can you come over to my house please and quickly, I'm in a terrible pickle" pleaded Emily.

"What's happened?" I asked

"It's that damned Alaska contraption, just get over here quickly" Emily replied.

I was intrigued and went straight over.

I arrived to find Emily at the door waiting for me.

She beckoned me in.

"Now before we go into the living room, please close the door as soon as you get in there" said Emily

"Why? What's happened?" I asked again

Emily then explained "You know I have that Alaska thing that phones and plays the music"

I nodded

"Well it was such a lovely morning that I opened my patio doors and lay on the settee. I decided that I would put the sound of birdsong on the Alaska box. It was so relaxing that I fell asleep" she explained

"So, what's the problem" I asked

"When I woke up the level of noise of the birdsong had increased significantly, to my horror the living room was like an avery. I have never seen so many birds. Now I don't know how to get them out." Said Emily "I can only assume that the birdsong on Alaska must have had mating calls included or something" she continued.

I went into the living room it was like a scene from the Hitchcock movie. Every bird you could imagine sitting on top of the lampshades the television and her curtain pole seemed a particular favourite.

The conundrum was how to get them out, we tried some bread and that shifted about ten birds who took the bait.

I did manage to throw a towel over a few and carry them out.

Finally, we decided to run the Alaska box out into the garden and play it at full volume, in the hope that the birds would be attracted to the mating calls as they were before.

Emily though said "Alaska play the Birdy Song" rather than Birdsong and all the neighbourhood where subjected to a very loud version the 1981 Tweets Birdy Song.

It certainly bought the neighbours out into their gardens. They must have thought she had gone mad.

But thankfully Emily quickly corrected her mistake and birdsong mating calls were blasting out of the Alaska box.

Fortunately this worked, apart from one stubborn pheasant which took a further half an hour to get out.

Why are those birds so stupid?

On the plus side the living room had to be thoroughly cleaned as there was bird mess everywhere, it must be the first time in years that anything had been cleaned in the house.

To give you some idea I found an Aztec chocolate bar wrapper behind the TV. This was last sold in 1978!

I arrived home four hours later, what a day.

Wednesday 1st April

Very dark outside

The clock had stopped in my bedroom at 3.45am, so I got up and went downstairs only to find that the actual time was 3.52am.

So back to bed, but I couldn't get back off to sleep as I had this stupid colon and endoscopy to go to this morning.

Just after dawn, I got up and had a bath.

I then paced up and down the living room for ages, I was so nervous that by 8.30am I was sweating so much I had to have shower.

Jane Roid said she would go with me, she is a good friend.

She picked me up later and off we set for the Hurtglands Hospital in her Clio.

We took an age to park at the hospital, and I started to panic as time was getting on.

Also the Endoscopy Department and the Colonoscopy Department seemed to be either end, of the Hospital that is!

As we were so near the appointment time, I plump for the Endoscopy Department and asked at reception.

At the reception, before I could even speak the receptionist said "Name?"

"Ramsbottom Ophelia" I replied

"Date of Birth" the receptionist enquired

I informed her of my date of birth and that's where things started to go wrong.

"Well we have nothing down under that name" she said

I informed her about the procedure I was to undertake.

"Blimey!" she said "Aren't you the unlucky one, try the Colonoscopy Dept, also best to start at the bottom and work your way up. That's what my dad always said!" she said with a giggle.

By this time, it was almost noon when I arrived at the Colonoscopy Department.

I went through the same procedure with the receptionist there, with the same reaction.

Finally, I gave her my appointment letter. The receptionist then got on the phone.

A huge queue had now built up behind me.

The receptionist returned. "Did you read this appointment letter in full?" she asked

"Well most of it" I replied

"Did you notice that the letter stated that you would be seeing a Doctor Maurice Dancer who would be assisted by a Nurse U Rerhyme." She asked with a smile.

"I think you have been had, it is April Fool's day after all" she said as she handed the letter back to me.

I looked at Jane Roid. "That bloody Major I'll kill him" I said

On the way home we stopped for a pub lunch at the Snakes Arms a small pub in the countryside.

Partly I was relieved that I didn't have to through the ordeal, partly mad at the Major, but eventually I did see the funny side after all he did make himself look a fool thinking he had won first prize in the National Trust draw last year.

I was glad when Jane dropped me off at home as I was very tired.

How on earth did I fall for that stupid prank, I must be getting old.

Thursday 2nd April

Sunny a nice day

I went for a walk this morning to the Two Stop shop. Mr Khan greeted me with a smile. "What can I get for you Mrs Ramsbottom not that I wish to probe of course unlike the NHS" he said and burst out laughing.

Once again, I am the butt of jokes in the Village.

Then the Major walked "By God Gal, your looking down in the mouth, but don't worry I have Nurse U

Rerhymes number if you want it" He laughed so much that his face went redder than the Tomatoes that were on display next to him.

"You wait until next year!" I replied and I left the shop clutching the milk and a loaf I had just bought.

As it is a nice day, I rang Emily and asked her if she fancied going to the National Thrust House Packemin Clinton.

This afternoon we set off for our visit to Packemin Clinton the old country house it was quite full when we arrived so we had a coffee and we decided to go on the "House Tour" at a later allotted time. This was the last tour of the day so there was only the two of us as most people had left.

Our tour guide John was a rotund man. He had a long ginger beard and had a strong Scottish accent. "Welcome to the Packemin Tour" he boomed as we walked in, he then turned to Emily and said in a whisper "Where you standing is the very spot that Lady Elizabeth Raleigh's succumbed to Walter's charms on 5th November 1590 allegedly. I bet that was a night to remember!" He said with a wink.

We were only in the hall way!

"Walter himself was known as Ruff Raleigh as it is believed he never took his ruff off!" The guide proclaimed raising one eyebrow. "Follow me" he said and walked off.

Then he went into the Lounge "This is the oldest part of the house if you look into the fire place and up the chimney you will see the initials FAR scratched into the brickwork. That is believed to be the initials of Father Angus Richard Truckminton the family Priest who hid up that chimney for a month. He was caught before he could finish adding the initial T for Truckminton. This being at the time of the Reformation in 1521. We can all be thankful he didn't complete it as that would have taken some explaining, people may of taken it as a command!" said John with a smile.

We then went into the Kitchen / Scullery. "That colander hanging above your head is said to be the very colander used to give Oliver Cromwell his infamous haircut prior to going into battle at Naseby in 1645." Explained John

From there we went upstairs and to the main bedroom. "The stain on the floor was believed to be the blood of Guy Faulks Sister, Dinah Faulks, she was murdered by her maid in this very room because Dinah had knocked over a chamber pot and asked the maid to clear it up. It was a very hard life for a maid and I assumed she had had enough, the poor girl was hanged in May 1600." John informed us.

"It is also believed that the term "Going potty" to describe someone going mad, originates from this incident, it is also where the term "Taking the P" comes from, as this is what the Maid is believed to have said prior to hitting Dinah over the head with the pot itself" stated John

"You said "Was?"" I said

"Was what?" replied John

"Was believed to be the blood of Dinah" I enquired

"Oh yes, we had the stain analysed in 1972 and it turned out to be beetroot juice!" said John

"Let's move on to the Secret Chapel" he continued

When we arrived in the Chapel, John again gave us his spiel again with as much poetic licence as he was allowed! "This Chapel was only discovered as recent as 1731. It was hidden behind a wooden panel and is believed to be haunted. It is said that on the 2nd April each year you can hear Monks chanting and in the distance the plucking of Sir Richard Grenville's Lute playing Greensleeves. With today being that very day, I will leave you in silence for a few minutes to listen and lament ladies for poor Richard, who is laid to rest under your very feet." John then disappeared leaving us in the dank semi-lit Chapel. It was very eerie.

After a few minutes the utter silence was suddenly broken as John poked his head around the door.

He shouted "Well that concludes the tour, have a lovely day"

We nearly wet ourselves we jumped that much from the shock of his booming voice.

We left the building like two giggling schoolgirls.

A much better day than yesterday.

Friday 3rd April

Sunny again unbelievable!

A quiet morning, I did give the lawn its first mowing of the year.

Why is it you put the mower away in October, making sure the electric flex is nice and tidy, yet when you get it back out again the flex has taken on the appearance of spaghetti junction.

Twenty minutes it took to untangle it!

This afternoon it was The Knit Wits meeting.

I walked in looking for Mrs Catterack to discuss her traffic light situation as I had heard she was getting very stressed about the actions we were taking.

Mrs Catterack was noticeable by her absence!

I asked Jane Roid if she had seen her. Her reply was not what I wanted to hear.

"You obviously haven't heard then" said Jane

"Heard what?" I asked

"Mrs Catterack overdosed her tablets this morning" said Jane

My heart sank, I felt dreadful this was all my doing"

Jane continued "Yes" she said "The home help found her this morning on the floor frothing everywhere."

"Oh dear" I said, I have never felt so low, I knew she was stressed, why do I always go in with all guns blazing. This is awful.

Jane continued her story "It was at this point the home help phoned emergency services, but the person she spoke to, said that he was out on another job and wouldn't be able to get there for the next hour or two"

That NHS I thought, it's getting ridiculous Mrs Catterack could be dead by then.

"So that's why she is not here today" said Jane quite matter of fact and walked off.

"But is she ok?" I said

"Yes, she's fine, apart from the mess to clear up" said Jane

"But you said she had taken an over dose" I said

Jane looked puzzled "No, she had over dosed the washing machine, she put four washing powder tablets in by mistake. The whole place is full of foam as the machine couldn't cope it has stopped working.

The emergency call out Guy, can't get there yet so she won't be here today." explained Jane.

"Why, what did you think I meant?"

"I thought she was dead" I replied

To which Jane went into hysterical laughter.

After Jane had calmed down she announced to the group that we have decided to knit balaclavas after all.

These will be red, amber and green and we will knit as many as we can for the protest about the traffic lights.

I even provided the wool, as I know what this lot are like, we would end up with all the colours of the rainbow otherwise.

Saturday 4th April

A miserable day.

National Chicken Cordon Bleu Day

I know I can't believe it either, it's a shame it isn't National Corn Beef and Pickle sandwich day as that's what I am having!

This morning it is painting day with Jan Gough, so I walked down to the Village Hall.

Jan seemed very excited this week we are covering "Pop Art"

"Think Andy Warhol. Think Campbells Soup, Think Marilyn Munro." Said Jan excitedly.

We were given the most vivid colours to work with.

"Now "said Jan "I don't want copies of Andy's work, I want originality in a pop art style" explained Jan.

On the table was a picture of Margaret Thatcher, another of the back of John Lennon's head, a very over ripe banana and a tin of sardines"

"Get to work you have one hour!" said Jan

I turned around and all that was left on the table was the tin of sardines, which had been half opened with a key.

I can only imagine how long they had been in someone's cupboard, I couldn't remember how long it was since I saw a key on a tin.

Apart from anything else the smell from the tin was overpowering.

The two artists either side of me moved the easels well away, and a few of my fellow artists rubbed Vick under their noses to mask the smell of the Sardines.

I tried to paint them but could hardly see the canvas as my eyes watered so much.

At the end of the hour my effort was given a score of three out of ten.

But at least that was better than Mrs Beaverbrook and Mrs Campbell as they had completely mis-understood the brief.

Mrs Beaverbrook had just drawn Matt Munro and Mrs Campbell had painted a Pop tart!

Later on, I watched an old episode of "Who wants to be Millionaire" it was the one where the contestant Cedric Plimsole was asked "In the

Nursery Rhyme Hickory Dickory Dock, What time did the clock strike when the mouse run up the clock" A Twelve O'clock, B Eleven O'clock, C Ten O'clock or D One O'clock. This was his first question for a £100.

You could see the fear in Cedric's eyes, he started to panic and instead of asking the audience he went fifty -fifty.

As he didn't know the answer that didn't help either, so he phoned a friend who lived in Argentina called Valentina? He didn't have a clue either surprisingly!

Finally he asked the audience, they helped Cedric out by giving him the correct answer. Cedric went on to win £8000 but all people remember is that opening disaster.

This reminded me of Patsy Sprat a girl from our very Village who appeared on "Blockbusters" with Bob Holness in 1985.

"What P has the currency Zloty?" asked Bob. Quick as a flash Patsy pressed her buzzer and shouted out "Poundland!"

Nobody remembers her brilliant answers referring to Latin and her knowledge of Greek Mythology, all that sticks are that answer "Poundland"

Children can be so cruel, poor Patsy didn't go to school for a month because of the ridicule, in fact that answer lowered her confidence and she under achieved all her life because of it. Such a shame.

I had a quiet night in watching Pants and Heck!
They seem to be on everything

Sunday 5th April

Warm and sunny.

Up early it is a beautiful morning.

I had Porridge for breakfast this morning the Major
had Kippers. Not that I am with the Major, but this
morning he decided to eat his breakfast on his Patio
and I was caught down wind of his garden.

I seem to be plagued by the smell of fish this
weekend!

Actually, I walked to Church with the Major this
morning as we left for Church at the same time.

I have set a date for the traffic light protest and the
Major is also available that day.

Father Aweigh greeted us both at the Church
entrance. "No speeches today Ophelia there isn't the
time" Father Aweigh instructed me.

During the service Father Aweigh stood up and
made an announcement.

"Brethren. Due to new legislation regarding Health
and Safety within the Church we have now to be
aware of the congregation's needs" announced the
Priest

I did wonder what the "congregations needs" could possibly be!

Father Aweigh continued. "Therefore, when taking Communion today there will be a choice of Communion bread and selection of wine. Now to make this easier for myself and my Presiders, I have produced a menu. Mrs Beaverbrook our Church Warden will hand these out for you to make you selection prior to coming to the alter rail, later in the service."

Mrs Beaverbrook then handed out the menu's pew by pew.

Well it is a world gone mad!

The Menu read

Body of Christ

Bread: White, Wholemeal, Gluten Free, Rye, Sourdough or Ezekiel

Blood of Christ

Wine: Pinot Noir, Fortified Sherry, Non-Alcoholic or Ribena Blackcurrant.

Please state which you wish to take on arrival at the alter rail.

If you are young looking please provide ID as proof of age prior to requesting the Blood of Christ,

Father Aweigh then went behind the Alter to commence the Service, it was only then I noticed the banquet in front of him.

The Alter had taken on the appearance of a Market Stall at the Snobihill Food Festival.

When the time come to take Communion, it was chaos as you can imagine.

Bernadette O'Leary was next to me at the alter rail and took an age deciding "I think I will try the Rye Father, I have seen it at Waitloads and always wondered what it tasted like!" said Bernadette.

The Lady the other side asked if she could have granary on the menu next week.

Another parishioner Mrs Clancy asked Father Aweigh "What do you recommend Father?"

Mr Tway asked if the Ribena was sugar free?

I thought it was never going to end.

Old Mr Crabtree got very confused and went home to get his birth certificate to prove his age.

The Service took in total two and half hours to complete, Communion alone took forty minutes.

There is too much choice in everything, I counted sixty-five different cheeses at the Waitloads deli counter last week. Sixty-five!

Why!

Monday 6th April

Another lovely day

Well I achieved the impossible this morning after months of trying to get that "Flossing" right.

I finally managed to accomplish it, all be it very slow.

I did try to speed the dance up but knocked a vase over and then fell over myself, but it's a start.

Emily called in this afternoon to practice her one line again.

Later we went down to the Drama Class at the Village Hall.

Everard and DRT greeted us at the door Everard was dressed in a bright yellow cat suit and DRT was dressed from top to toe in red velvet, even his shoes.

"I assume Dipsy and Tinky Winky are inside, are they?" I said laughing.

They both looked at each other and shrugged not having a clue what I was going on about.

I suggested to Everard that the competitive dance routine, where the Shirts "Floss" and the Vests "Twerk" should be slowed down, and it would be all the funnier for it.

To my amazement after a lengthy discussion with DRT, he agreed! Such a relief, hopefully now I won't humiliate myself.

The evening went very well as we went through the whole play again.

Everard got his Yamaha organ out, it was quite impressive.

Once again, a very excited Everard shouted "Sing my angels sing" as he tried to reach for a semi-quaver while his fingers danced over the keyboard.

The lyrics though, still leave something to be desired.

The songs were from West Side Story but the lyrics were certainly not!

Somethings Coming now became Somethings Humming!

Maria was now Diarrhoea (I've just had a bout of Diarrhoea)

America was now Formica sang by my good self. I like the smell of Formica etc.

Tonight, was still Tonight, but the first line was Tonight, Tonight, there will be no Dole tonight, Tonight there will be no Daily Star!

Gee- Officer Krapknee. Emily's big number, consisting of one line!

I Feel Pretty now I Feel Witty followed by every itty you can think of!

One Hand, One Heart was now One Burp, One Fart.

Finishing off with There's a Plaice for Us.

Tony dies in the final scene after being stabbed by a wooden fork at the local Chippy.

Although how that gets through Wayne's Donkey Jacket still remains a mystery!

One more rehearsal to go before the big night, I am already starting to get nervous.

Tuesday 7th April

Drizzle and Misty. It sounds like a double act!

Well for once I was looking forward to the day ahead.

It is the U3A Meeting this afternoon and for a change it is something interesting.

We are re-enacting a court room drama from a crime committed in 1961.

A retired Judge, Judge Grinder is keeping proceedings in order and I have been selected at random to be on the jury.

I have never been called for jury service so this is probably as close as I will get. I am so excited.

I have been practicing saying the line "We find the defendant guilty your Honour"

I walked down to the Village Hall this afternoon with the Major.

"I hope you're not open to bribes Rammy" he said with a chuckle.

When we arrived, the hall was packed and there at the side near the front were twelve empty chairs ready and waiting for the Jury.

Judge Grinder took the twelve of us into a small room. He stated that we must hear all the evidence and the defence before reaching a verdict. "This is a murder trial so the consequences will be extreme if the defendant is found guilty. This is as it would be in 1961." Said Judge Grinder.

Well my heart was pounding as we were led in front of everyone in the hall to our seats.

The downside was in fact the Jury members, as well myself there was some familiar faces, Mr Crabtree, Miss Everton, Mrs Tushingham, Mr Khan and thankfully Jane Roid, who I sat next to.

I didn't recognise the other six.

A spokesperson was elected by a lottery and unfortunately that fell to Mr Crabtree.

We then were instructed to all rise as Judge Grinder entered the room.

Finally, the Defendant was bought in. Brad Ford Shufflecock played this role, he is Billy's Shufflecock's brother.

Known throughout the Village as Brad Ford (Fingers) Shufflecock as he was caught stealing a Sherbet Dib Dab at the Two Stop Shop when aged only seven years. This Village never forgets, that incident was fifteen years ago!

He was named Brad Ford as he was conceived in Bradford apparently when his parents went on a tour of Yorkshire in their old Skoda, although from what I have heard it would have been more accurate if Brad had been called Hatchback!

As soon as "Fingers" Shufflecock walked in Mr Crabtree stood up and shouted "Guilty your Honour!"

Mr Crabtree was told to sit down by the Court Usher.

The case was then read out to "Fingers" Shufflecock who played the part of the defendant Hugh Watt who was accused of murder in 1961.

On the 2nd January 1961, Hugh killed his wife Norah Watt by belting her over the head with his Spotty Dick!

In his defence, all that Norah could cook was suet-based meals.

If it wasn't Spotty Dick it was Rolly Polly, Dumplings or very occasionally Steak and Kidney Pudding. Sadly, though this never included any steak or kidney as she didn't know how to cook that!

Hugh Watt eventually snapped after years of a suet diet.

This was a difficult case, I think I would crack if I had years of suet, but surely he could have cooked himself something?

As the case went on, we did learn that Norah was a very dominant woman. Hugh was only allowed in the kitchen to wash up and dry the crocks. Whoa betide Hugh if that wasn't done right.

He had also been admitted into hospital in December 1960 after an incident with a Black Pudding. He had naively brought the Black Pudding home one evening for his tea. Norah was not happy!

All the evidence was taken into account and we were asked to deliberate on our verdict.

Myself and the rest of the Jury retired to a room at the side of the main hall.

Mr Crabtree couldn't seem to grasp that this wasn't about "Fingers" Shufflecock.

He said "Perhaps he stole the Sherbet Dib Dab because he was fed up of Suet!

We ignored him as we only had ten minutes to make up our minds.

We then went back into the Hall.

The Usher then asked us for our verdict.

Mr Crabtree stood up and said in a loud clear voice, "We find Fingers guilty your Judgeness"

Judge Grinder then put a black cloth on his head and sentenced "Fingers" alias Hugh Watt to be taken from this place and hanged"

It was so realistic Mrs Shufflecock, Fingers Mom, screamed.

Miss Everton fainted.

Even "Fingers" himself looked worried.

Then Judge Grinder stood up, and thanked us all for taking part.

"In the real case Hugh Watt was sentenced to twelve years for Manslaughter on the grounds of diminished responsibility" Judge Grinder announced "I was surprised that you the Jury were so severe!" he said shaking his head.

I felt dreadful and you could feel distain for us in the room. You would have thought we had committed the Murder.

Wednesday 8th April

Fresh and Breezy.

Terrible wind in the night kept me awake, so I am very tired this morning.

Emily phoned this morning, she was very excited.

"As we aren't going to the slimming at the moment, I have found the ideal substitute. You will love it! I will pick you up at 1pm!" stated Emily then put the phone down.

"What Now", I said to myself as I replaced the receiver.

I have no idea where we are going or what I should wear. I settled for smart casual a posh blouse and Jeans.

Emily arrived at 12.35pm tooting her horn over and over again.

"Your early!" I said as I got into the car.

"I know but I wanted to get a seat near the front" said Emily

"Where are we going?" I asked

"Didn't I say" said Emily "It's Poetry Corner in Snobihill"

"I am certainly not a poet" I said

"Exactly" said Emily "They teach you"

"If you keep driving like this, we will be dead. You have just gone over a traffic light on red" I said

"See you're a natural" said Emily laughing.

We arrived in the Snobihill and went into the venue. Immediately I felt uncomfortable. About thirty heads all swivelled around and looked at the pair of us.

A man approached us. "Hello I'm Cedric" he said, He was wearing a tweed jacket, flouncy shirt and a blue cravat. He had an empty pipe hanging from the corner of his mouth. "Do take a seat. For the first twenty minutes Members read their poems and then we analyse the prose. Afterwards we discuss topics for the following week. It's just about to start"

I looked at Emily and shook my head as we both took our seats. She could see I was annoyed.

Then a young lady dressed in black leather and sporting a lovely bright pink Mohican appeared at the front and faced us, Poem in hand.

"This is called Transfusion" she said after taking chewing gum out of her mouth, the young lady then began to read.

My life was full of confusion

My life was full of disillusion

My life I thought, had reached its conclusion

Until I had that transfusion!"

After a pause, the members went into rapturous applause.

Then the young lady who was dressed in clothing from the "World of Leather!" sat down.

Another Lady then stood up.

"Hello I'm Agatha. I have written a poem which reminds me of my Mom who sadly passed away last year"

"It's called "The Past""stated Agatha and then read her poem.

The Past doesn't last before it is taken.

You yearn for just a day, when you could reclaim it.

But alas! No, your wish is forsaken.

If only the good times could be recalled in your mind.

You long for a hand or voice from the past.

Please grant me a day, a minute with the one, I long to find.

But the past gets no nearer just further away.

The past gets more selfish with each passing day.

As the past takes your memories and locks them away!

Agatha left the stage looking very upset, while the audience applauded.

I was in tears myself as was Emily, what a cheery afternoon this was turning out to be.

The rest of the poems were all quite depressing, apart from one a poem about a running nose.

Running nose, running nose why don't you stop?

Running nose, running nose always full of snot.

Running nose, running nose, what am I to do?

Running nose, how do I cease this endless green glue?

Running nose, is this what has become of me, now I'm seventy-two?

Even that had a ring of truth about it.

I have never felt so down after a day out.

We both just stared into our cups of tea afterwards at the Coff and Drop Café. Emily and I sat in silence, me thinking about my Mother and Emily thinking about Joe her Cocker Spaniel both now sitting in heaven hopefully.

I don't think we will go again.

Thursday 9th April

Cold and a Frost. Will this winter ever end?

This evening it is the meeting about the traffic lights and humping of our High Street.

I have been phoning around all morning getting support, and everyone I phoned said they would be there. Fingers crossed.

I have knitted two balaclavas in red, amber and green for myself and Emily to wear.

I have also got all the TCP T-shirt's for sale. Life seems to have a purpose again.

 Well my feeling of optimism was short lived went the phone rang. It was Wayne.

"Hi Mrs O, I've got Lardys funeral date from Fat Berg. It's tow wecks today. 11am at the Burntwood Crem. now flowers, just downations to the "Mr Kipplin Foundation"" he said laughing, Nah not really, downations to Cancer Research." Said Wayne "Mus gu"

On that he put the phone down.

Later on this evening I walked down to the Village Hall for the meeting. To my amazement it was packed, so much so I had an attack of nerves, I don't like standing up and talking, well not to this many people.

I stood on the stage and informed every one of my plans.

"We will meet at the Village Hall on Saturday morning at 10.45am. Then we will walk down to the traffic lights outside Mrs Catterack's house.

"Blocking the road is our priority until the police come and move us.

I want banners, placards. musical instruments, and lots of noise.

Please wear red, amber or green outfits on Saturday.

This is an injustice that needs to be made right." I shouted to the crowd before me.

The Knit Wits Group had done themselves proud and produced twenty balaclavas albeit being all one colour but that didn't matter.

"All proceeds from the T-shirts and balaclavas will go towards Mrs Catterack's legal fees should this be needed" I announced.

I received rapturous applause.

The T-shirt's were sold within minutes as were the balaclavas.

By the end of the evening we had raised £488 pounds for Mrs Catterack.

Did I feel good! Can't wait for Saturday.

Friday 10th April

Hot and Humid

National Hug your Dog day.

I have just got to find a dog now!

Tonight, we are going to Snobihill Theatre to see Flack and Decker Workmates.

Tomorrow is the protest so I need to look good!

I phoned up Gail's Nails and asked Gail to come over this morning?

Fortunately, Gail informed me that the Major had just cancelled his monthly pedicure.

Gail explained "Well I say pedicure, it's more of a battle with his feet. He has got bigger corns than the Jolly Green Giant. See yers lata" with that she put the phone down.

Pedicure the Major? You think you know somebody? I thought to myself.

Gail arrived at 11.13am a minute late. No sooner in the house Gail was off on one "There's a load of angry people owt there, I know because I am painting a lot of red nails and puttin in loads of studs"

Said Gail. "Yam got em all riled, with your speeches, yow shud run for Mayor"

Gail tidied me up and painted my nails red, amber and green, ready for tomorrow.

After a quiet afternoon, Emily arrived with fish and chips.

Later we set off for the Theatre in Emily's car and a very strange thing occurred or should I say didn't occur.

We braked several times but the horn didn't toot once? It's hard to believe but I think Emily has lost weight.

On arrival at the Theatre security was completely over the top.

Bag's where checked then I was frisked by a huge lady, when she had finished, she had lost a glove. We never did find it?

Finally, security got one of those wands that detect knives.

It went ballistic when it was waved over Emily's breasts. Well that caught everyone's attention.

Several people had already assembled at the fire assembly point outside, thinking the fire alarm had gone off.

I thought she had still got the weights in her bra that she had at the Slimming Club.

Emily very reluctantly explained that she was wearing an iron corset!

"For medicinal purposes, I have a bad back" she revealed.

I looked at her with a knowing look, she knew, I knew that she didn't have a bad back at all.

Thankfully they let us both in. I have no idea what that was all about.

We found our seats, Emily then explained about the iron corset. "I bought it on ebay. I thought it said "No Iron Corset", so I bought it thinking I wouldn't have to iron it. It actually said "No 1 Iron Corset."

I believed her thousands wouldn't! It did explain why her car horn didn't toot.

Dumind Decker the Desmond Decker Tribute came on and was very good. Singing "The Israelites" and "You can get it, if you really want" he was very good.

Just before the interval Dumind made an announcement "The reason for the extra security is because this afternoon someone found a piece of paper in my Dressing Room that stated "Persecution you must fear. Win or lose. You will get your share". The theatre staff took no chances and increased security.

It is only after singing "You can get it if you really want" that I realised that those words on the note are lyrics from that song. I must have dropped them" Said Dumind "Sorry" he said.

All that commotion for nothing.

The second half it was Roberta Flock the Roberta Flack Tribute.

It would have been good except for the fact that Roberta had trouble when pronouncing an S.

Not sure if it was Roberta or Roberta's dentures that was the problem but whistling on ever S was hard to listen to.

"Killing me Sssssoftly" was ruined as was "The first time ever I Ssssaw your face".

Otherwise she did sound like her.

She was joined by Dumind Decker for the last few songs. They sang three Motown numbers.

Although why they chose the Four Tops Hit "Sssstanding in the Sssshadows of love" I will never know!

Saturday 11ᵗʰ April

Sunny this morning thank goodness.

I woke up so early this morning with a mixture of interpretation and excitement.

I checked I had everything I needed for the protest. I have made a placard with "Justice for Hampton" on it.

I am wearing a red, yellow and green balaclava a "No TCP on my Little Hampton" T-shirt with a yellow skirt and green tights. I looked hideous and prayed I would not be alone in this campaign.

At 10.25 am. I made my way to the Village Hall.

I was amazed as I approached the Village Hall as there must have been over fifty people standing outside. They cheered as I arrived, all of them waving their placards in the air. It was a mass of red, yellow and green, this was such a relief.

The Major, Mr Tway, Mrs Catterack, Bernadette O'Leary, Wendy Miller, Jane Roid, Miss Everton and Wayne were all there to name just a few.

"Come on Gal, let's march!" said the Major.

We slowly walked down the High Street past the Two Stop Shop where I noticed Mr Khan had boarded his windows up.

"I have seen these protests before, they always smash the shop windows" said Mr Khan as we passed by his shop.

Looking at the age of the protesters, I would be surprised if anyone could lift a brick never mind throw one.

As we approached the traffic lights outside Mrs Catterack's house we had already moved into the road. Five cars were tooting their horns as we held up the traffic.

Once there we sat down in the road, Mr Tway produced his five miles of French knitting and everyone tied themselves to the person next to them. Mobility scooters also stretched across the road.

It was quite a blockade.

Mrs Tushingham produced five sets of fluffy handcuffs, no one dare ask where those had come from!

Within half an hour the local newspapers reporters from the Hampton Bugle and the Snobihill Star were both there taking photographs and interviewing the protesters.

After forty-five minutes the Police arrived but we refused to move. They seemed unsure what to do.

After an hour three Caravans had been set up selling food, "Snack Donalds", "Burger Off" and a Jacket Potato man called "Mash in the Static"

A large crowd had also gathered to watch. Traffic was at a standstill. The difficulty the Police had was untangling all the Zimmer frames that had been chained together.

By 1pm the local TV arrived and started filming and interviewing.

Two O'clock it started raining so we called it a day. I think we have made our point though and that's what counts.

As we all started walking home, Mr Crabtree arrived with his placard which read "Stop making Pelican's and Zebras cross!"?

"Is it over? I thought it was 2.45pm start" he said

Thank goodness it is!

But we did make the evening News. Presenter Owen Nicks stating our case.

It was a good day and fortunately no-one got arrested.

Sunday 12th April

Still raining.

I walked to church this morning even before I got into the church, I was being congratulated and thanked by so many people.

I didn't really know what to do, no-one has ever appreciated me, so praise does not come very easy for me to take.

Once in the Church, Father Aweigh asked me to say a few words.

I went to the front and stood at the Lectern. I explained what had happened, although in this Village I am sure everyone knew already.

I also explained that we will now give it a week, and hopefully some action will be taken regarding Mrs Catterack's electricity.

"If not, we will do it all again." I shouted banging my fist on the Lectern.

Once again, the congregation applauded some punching the air.

Father Aweigh soon intervened as he thought it was getting out of hand.

The sermon was very apt in was the story of the "Good Samaritan" although "David and Goliath" may have been more appropriate.

I had my lunch alone again. The traditional Sunday lunch is a thing of the past, when cooking for one!

Today I had whatever was left in the fridge. So today I had sprats, spam and a scotch egg.

It's a good job Roberta Flock doesn't have to order that for lunch with all those S's on the menu!

I stopped in and watched TV for the rest of the day.

Having watched "The Canal Trip" in actual time on BBC 4, a few months ago and the "Bus Journey" last week.

Both sent me to sleep I hasten to add. I thought I would give the latest programme a viewing.

"A Cows eye view!" Well I was only an hour in and once again I was nodding off. Nothing happened!

The cow stood in a field for an hour, then lay down for an hour. Finally, after two and a half hours, we had some action at last when the cow went in for milking. Even then, once in the milking parlour the cow faced the wall for half an hour.

The programme was on for four hours in total, what a waste of my licence fee.

The trouble is once you have committed to this sort of programme, you are spell bound and feel obliged to keep watching just in case something happens.

You can only imagine how excited I got when a squirrel ran across the field, two hours in!

What a boring day after yesterday.

Monday 13th April

Showers (Your love comes in showers)

It always reminds me of that song. If only I could remember what that song is?

It's National Scrabble Day.

I said there was a day for everything, Emily's coming over later so hopefully we will fit a game in.

It is the final rehearsal this evening for our production of "Back Side Story". I am getting more and more nervous.

I tried to master the flossing this morning and practised singing my song "I love the smell of Formica"

Lord knows what the neighbours think.

Emily arrived this afternoon and we did play Scrabble. The defining moment was Emily thinking she had won the game playing Quart only for me to play my Z and Y on a triple word with Quartzy.

I thought she was going to kick the board up in the air.

Later we ambled down to our last rehearsal at the Village Hall.

Everard greeted us dressed in blue and red striped shirt and trousers to match.

He was though being supported by a pair of wooden crutches. He looked like a deck chair.

"What happened to you?" I asked Everard.

"I was showing DRT my fandango and I over stretched my rectus femoris" explained Everard.

Once we were inside the Hall. DRT pirouetted onto the stage. He too was dressed in stripes but he was in yellow and orange.

I feel like I am on the set of Playschool!

"Thespians, I have a few changes to make" announced Dave Revell Tallwood

This got our attention. "As Wayne seems very reluctant to discard his Horse Coat" said DRT

"Ya mean Donkey Jacket" Wayne corrected him.

"Yes that. Well we, Everard and I thought that it would be a good idea if all the gang of Vests wore a Hors.. a Donkey Jacket, so we have hired some for you to wear. Also the dance off between the Vests and Shirts will not now be in slow motion." stated DRT.

Everard and I think the slow mo twerking is far too raunchy for Little Hampton." Explained DRT

"So we will do it normal speed, we do though have strobe lighting which we will use appropriately as we do not want to offend anyone" said Everard

"Great!" I thought "I can only floss slowly, with the strobe, I will just look like I am just twitching"

The night when ok, but there was a lot of condensation on the windows from the amount of sweat created due to the Vests wearing the Donkey Jackets.

I sang ok. Cordelia (Maria) sang beautifully as did Wayne.

DRT and Everard got very emosh at the end.

Everard then made one final announcement "No rehearsal next Monday, Jan Gough is here all next week touching up her husband's very impressive Empire State Building and finishing off the rest of the scenery. Break a Leg everyone!" shouted Everard waving his crutch in the air, he then fell over.

So that's it. Rehearsals are done.

A week on Friday and Saturday are the big nights. They are already sold out!

Tuesday 14th April

Foggy then Sunny.

Another lovely day eventually.

I got two slices of bread out from one of Mr Khans loaves this morning and one was already toasted! Who's doing this?

I was thinking this morning about last night and the strobe lighting.

My Grandfather Bill always maintained that it was because of his actions that the strobe light was invented.

In the year 1917, He tested light bulbs at a factory. All he had to do was put them in a socket and if they lit up, he passed them to his young workmate Harold, who would pack the bulbs in a box.

Bill was so adept at this he could test bulbs at such a fast rate it created a strobe effect.

So much so that the poor Harold looked like he was working in slow motion and was duly sacked for shirking!

That person according to my Grandfather was Harold Edgerton who later became a Doctor and in 1931 invented the strobe light.

I think he was making it up, but you never know.

I loved Grandfather Bill Weaklea so much. I must stop getting melancholy!

I phoned Jane Roid up and asked her if she fancied going into Snobihill as I needed a new top.

Later we arrived in Snobihill and went for a coffee, from there we went looking around the clothes shops ending up outside the clothes shop "Merde Vêtements" surprisingly it had a closing down sale.

"Well I'm not surprised it's closing down with that name for the shop!" said Jane

My french is as good as nothing, the only french I know is "deux magnum blanc" which is great if you fancy an ice cream but not much good for anything else.

"What name?" I asked puzzled.

"Look it up!" said Jane laughing.

No joy with the clothes, nothing that's in fashion suits me, most of the styles out now I wore forty years ago and certainly do not want to wear them again.

Jane and I dropped into Waitloads supermarket before coming home. I fancied corn beef hash for tea so I waited at the deli counter.

Ahead of Jane and I was a very attractive elderly man who had the look of George Clooney about him.

"Could I have the six ounces of the extra thick ham thinly cut please?" said the Man

The woman serving was not amused. "I think this is the only ham available but I will ask" she said and then disappeared.

He turned to us and winked.

The women serving then re-appeared with a large ham hock in her hand. "How thin do you want it?"

She asked placing the ham on the meat slicer.

"The thickness of a sixpence" said the man

You could see she was getting annoyed. The women cut the ham and put it in a bag.

"Have you any Red Gloucester cheese? "asked the Man

"No! Do you mean Double Gloucester or Red Leicester?" She enquired

"Not Sure, I had it last week, it was served by Lorraine." said the man

"Wait there I will go and ask Lorraine" said the Lady and promptly dis-appeared again.

He turned again to us and winked.

To be honest I was getting fed up.

A few minutes later the lady returned again with Lorraine.

"No. I have never seen him before" stated Lorraine.

The man then said "No, the cheese served was next to the quiche lorraine"

"Are you winding us up?" said Lorraine

"No sorry it's on my shopping list, I am getting for my friend. He replied showing them the list.

"The last item is "unicorned beef" please, four slices?"

Both ladies now looked at him in dis-belief. They were so angry.

"I'm sorry were right out, can I serve the lady behind you please" said the Lady behind the counter.

The man said "Of course" and stood to one side.

The trouble was I wanted "corned beef" too!

I got a little flustered and said "Could I have a unit of corned beef please?" which did sound like "unicorned beef" Lord knows why I asked for a unit as a measure, I think I was in a state of panic.

Everyone stopped and looked at me. The lady behind the counter said "Are you two a double act?" pointing at me and the man.

Then the manager came over as the queue was starting to build. He took one look at me and said. "I know this lady she upset Mrs Pengleton-Smithe last time she was in the shop" he said.

"Will you please leave?" he said and pointed to the door.

The man who had caused all this commotion walked out of the shop with myself and Jane.

Once outside he apologised to us and then said. "It's Ophelia Lambs bottom, isn't it?"

"Ramsbottom" I replied.

"I recognise you from the protest last weekend., it was on the local news.

I am a TV producer. We are doing a programme shortly called "Pillars of our community".

It's based on heroic people in the local area and I would love to interview you" stated the man

"I will get my team to contact you, if that's ok?" he enquired.

I replied "Yes please" no idea why I said please.

"Great, we will set it up" he said. He then kissed the back of my hand.

"What's your name?" I asked as he started to walk away.

"Harry Stottle! We will be in touch" he shouted and disappeared.

Jane looked at me and just said "Harry Stottle?" shaking her head.

Not sure what to think now?

A strange day.

Wednesday 15th April

Squally showers

Not a good night's sleep I was tossing and turning all night. I couldn't stop thinking about Harry Stottle and yesterdays nightmare.

Then that name registered Pengleton-Smythe!

She is my daughter in Back Side Story. Maria! She is played by Cordelia Pengleton-Smythe in the drama.

Could it be their daughter? Not that it makes any difference I suppose.

The phone then rang, like a fool I dashed to pick it up thinking it was the TV Producer. Sadly, I trod on an upturned electric plug in my bare feet.

I let out a scream, just as I picked up the phone.

It was Emily "My God, are you alright?" she asked sounding concerned.

"No, I am not" I replied. Kicking the plug towards the skirting board.

"That's good!" said Emily obviously not listening to a word I said.

"Bob has given me two free tickets for the "Flower Show" at the NEC tomorrow as he couldn't go. Would you like to go, it's the biggest flower show in the Country apparently?"

Having always wanted to go to the "Chelsea Flower Show" and never being able to for one reason or another, the thought of this show really excited me.

My throbbing foot seemed to get better instantly.

"I would love to go" I replied

"Great, I will pick you up at 10am" said Emily and put the phone down.

I walked down to the Two Stop shop later. As I entered the shop I was confronted by a huge sign "Damaged goods reduced. Everything must go!"

I stood under the sign, looking at the battered boxes of Cornflakes, various dented tins and loaves of bread that looked like they had been run over by a steam roller.

The shop door then opened and the Major walked in, he took one look at me under the sign and shouted at the top of his voice "I don't care what's damaged about you Rammy, I am going to make Angus Khan an offer for you!"

He then turned to Mr Khan and shouted "How much for the Old Gal in the corner".

There was raucous laughter in the shop.

"More than you will ever afford" I said trying to get back some dignity in what was a packed shop.

I paid for a very dented tin of corned beef and walked out.

Made a hash of the hash this evening. It wasn't as nice as I thought it was going to be.

Thursday 16th April

Drizzling and heavy rain forecast.

Up early this morning as I was so excited about the flower show. Hopefully I can get some advice as my Squirrel Nutkin isn't what it was. Perhaps I should get a substitute rabbit just in case it's beyond repair. Thats if they have a topiary section.

I was also hoping that some celebrity gardeners may be there.

Dead on 10am Emily's horn tooted four times, so I assumed the iron corset was not being worn today!

We arrived at the NEC Birmingham twenty minutes later. Parking for the day was an extortionate £20, but Emily knew another car park that was £3.50 all day, so we parked there.

There was a reason it was so cheap. If we had walked from home, we would have been nearer!

After forty-five minutes we actually entered the NEC, even then Hall 1 was miles away.

We both tentatively stepped onto the travellator, which was crammed with what appeared to be chefs. This I found strange?

The Travellator seemed to be going so slow, so much so that the people walking along side it were going faster and passing us by.

The trouble was you couldn't get off the thing.

Then it sped up and we passed the walkers that had just passed us. We gave them the same smug look they had previously given us.

The travellator started going a bit too fast though and both Emily and I gave each other that knowing look that something wasn't quite right.

The Chefs were now holding onto their hats as we sped towards Hall 1 at about twenty miles an hour.

Then it varied its speed alternating between fast and very slow, we passed the same people walking along side us about ten times as they did us.

Finally, we got off at Hall 1, both Emily and I were feeling quite queasy.

The Chef's walked past us and went into Hall 1?

Emily and I queued with the rest of the crowd, eventually getting in. It was now noon, two hours since I left home!

Once in the Exhibition Hall I looked around for the flowers and show gardens.

Not one could be seen, just a load of bakers and chefs. There were loads of display stands even a windmill but no garden in front of it.

"Where are the flowers?" I asked Emily

"I don't know" she replied

"You did say "Flower Show"" I said

"Yes" replied Emily looking at the tickets

 "Oh No, it's flour as in baking!" Emily replied.

"It's an exhibition of the finest flour from around the world and the culinary delights they produce" explained Emily

Bob the baker gave me his tickets as he couldn't attend this year. He thought we would be interested" she said.

"Interested...Why would we be interested. It's flour?" I said.

The rest of the day was mainly spent drinking coffee and eating various types of bread and cakes while sitting outside the Dreggs bakery stand.

It wasn't such a bad day after all, apart from the fact everyone was covered in a dusting of flour as it lingered in the air.

Then we remembered that we had along jaunt home, we had both forgotten about the walk back to the car.

When we arrived in the car park Emily couldn't find the car. Half an hour we spent looking. Emily eventually ended up standing on a bin while I pressed the fob, both hoping to see her car indicators flash.

Home by 7.30 pm!

Friday 17th April

Sunny. Good Friday

I did go to Church this morning as it is the "Stages of the cross". There wasn't a great number of parishioners attending today though.

After an hour I realised why, this is a long service. Fourteen stages each with its own prayers.

Although I was glad I did attend the service by the end as it was nice to sit and reflect.

Afterwards there was an Easter egg hunt for the children.

That didn't go so well, Mrs Ravenbrook's four-year-old grandchild Cecilia walked into the church clutching what looked like three actual bird's eggs.

Mr Tway immediately identified them as very rare white and black speckled Hawfinch eggs.

To be fair to Cecilia it wasn't really her fault.

But Mr Tway was almost in a panic being a lifelong Twitcher himself. To be honest I have never seen him twitch so much! "Have you any idea how rare these are? The Hawfinch is one of the rarest birds in the UK. Where did you find them?" Mr Tway asked the little girl but she had no idea. "Somewhere over there" Cecilia said pointing to a long hedge at the edge of the graveyard.

Mr Tway wrapped the eggs in a warm tea towel and we all went out to search for the empty nest.

An hour later after getting my arms torn to shreds from the Hawthorn hedge. Nothing was found.

Mr Tway looked very concerned and to his horror when he opened the tea towel two of the eggs had cracked. It was then he noticed the melted chocolate oozing slightly from the cracked eggs.

"I am terribly sorry" he said "I seem to have made a mistake, I think they are Cadbury Mini eggs after all."

He then Googled the Hawfinch eggs to justify his mistake and they did look similar.

Even so myself and the rest of the search party were none too pleased. Mr Tway looked very embarrassed.

The Major didn't mince his words. "Take "cher" off the word Twitcher and do you know what you're left with? "Twit" otherwise known as "Mr Bloody Tway"" he shouted

Father Aweigh thanked everyone and managed to calm things down. Otherwise we would certainly have seen another fourteen stages of the Major being cross!

As we all left, I noticed to my horror, the poster on the Church notice board. It was advertising the Easter Fete tomorrow at the Village Hall. The poster background was my self-portrait painting of "The Scream". The details of the Fete were written over my painting but even so it was obviously me.

"My God Gal, that wasn't your best day was it!" said the Major as we all walked passed the notice board.

"I'm looking forward to seeing the original tomorrow" he continued laughing.

The rest of the day was nice and quiet, I practiced my lines and sang my song for Back Side Story.

I then fell asleep watching television and woke up at midnight, I hate doing that.

It was then I noticed about six messages on my phone, all saying more or less the same thing.

"Have you seen this weeks Hampton Bugle?"

I don't get the Bugle until tomorrow as Mr Tussock takes so long with delivery. It takes him two days.

Difficulty sleeping now, I just know tomorrow isn't going to be a good day.

Saturday 18th April

Sunny again

I was awoken at 5.30am this morning by the rattling of my letter box, but I was so tired having not got off to sleep until 3.30am that I went back to sleep.

Up at 9.30. As I went into the hall there laying on the carpet was the Hampton Bugle.

The headline read "Soil and Trouble" below the word "Soil" was a portrait picture of a man or should I say "Frankenstein" as that's what he looked like. Under the word "Trouble" was my headshot, I was wearing the red, yellow and green balaclava I had worn at the protest meeting last week. I looked ridiculous.

Then below was the report. "Council hit by two protests". "Council house cockney cleaner, Harry Hap, 34 years old, married with nine children. Known to fellow workers as "Flash Harry" due to him being so adept with his mop, was arrested this week.

Regarding the defecation of the toilet, Police are still looking into it. The Police would not comment further other than to say that Harry Hap was helping with their enquiries."

The second protest was a human road block at Little Hampton, led by revolting pensioner Ophelia Ramsbottom.

Fifty residents blocked the road in protest against the street lights in Little Hampton on the Rise.

Residents want the traffic calming prevented too, this is set to go ahead in June.

Their "No TCP (Traffic Calming Please) on my Little Hampton" campaign will continue if the Council do not back down" stated Campaign leader Red Ramsbottom.

And so it went on.

So once again it's me who is at the brunt of everything.

Later I went down to the Village Hall to see the Jan Gough Art Exhibition.

All of our work so far this year was on display. I saw the Major ahead of me looking at the artwork.

The lady with him said "That giant peach, is very good."

The Major looked at the painting and replied "I think that may be me, when I posed in the Life Class!"

"Oh, my goodness" said the lady "And is that one you too?" she said pointing at another painting.

The Major looked long and hard at the painting she referred to, "No" he replied looking a little disappointed "I think that is the Tower of Pisa" but I can check if you like?" stated the Major.

My picture "The Scream" was there larger than life, under a banner "Portrait of the Year"

Everyone was very kind and gave me pats on the back and many congratulations.

Such accolade made me forget about just how hideous I looked in the painting.

Apart from Father Aweigh who just said "It was very brave of you, painting yourself like that!"

Once again, I was filled with self-doubt.

Considering everyone must have seen the headlines in the Hampton Bugle no-one said anything. Not even the Major.

I think they all felt sorry for me.

Sunday 19th April

Raining

This morning I went to the Easter sunday service at Church.

For some reason Father Aweigh was not there when I arrived. Everyone wondered what to do, eventually Mrs Beaverbrook went to his house and arrived just as Father Aweigh was coming out of his front door.

He arrived at Church half an hour late looking very flustered.

As the Priest walked in the Major shouted, "Alleluia, he has risen indeed!"

I thought that was a bit harsh.

The service went ok, the sermon was cut short which was no bad thing although once again the Communion went on forever. Granary Bread and Ciabatta Bread had now been added to the bakery on the alter.

Afterwards I stayed for a cup of tea, Mr Crabtree managed to corner me.

"Still no Mrs Crabtree then?" I enquired.

"Well not today, she is crab sailing this morning" he explained "Then this afternoon she is gliding on a parrot or some out. She said she wanted to get that shopping list done before she has her ninetieth birthday next year." Said Mr Crabtree.

This took some working out, I can only assume it was abseiling and paragliding, but it would be funny if he was right.

Home for a meal for one, but like so many people my age this is how it is.

Easter used to be like Christmas but not anymore.

I received a text this afternoon from my friend Brenda who lives in Spain which read "Thanks very much!"

Poor Brenda had lost her husband a few weeks ago, I had sent her a "Happy Birthday" message yesterday, but when I read my message back, I was horrified.

Instead of texting "Happy Birthday, have a lovely day x" I had text "Happy Birthday have a lonely day x"

Now reading her text back does it mean a genuine "Thanks very much" or does it mean an annoyed "Thanks very much" with a hint of sarcasm.

No kiss either! What does that mean?

Now I am beating myself up, do I text again or will that highlight the fact that she is lonely.

In the end I did nothing, it was so much simpler when we phoned each other.

Songs of Praise this evening looked back at the history of the programme which began in 1961.

I remembered that first programme.

There was so little to do on a Sunday afternoon in the sixties. No shops, no sport, no take aways and even the pubs closed for most of the day. This is why "Points of View" with Robert Robinson had about eight million people watching it!

Monday 20th April

Raining

I hate Bank Holidays, everyone sees their families. There are no Clubs to go to, and basically nothing to do.

It was so bad that I started to spring clean!

Thankfully Emily came to the rescue and asked if I wanted to go to the cinema.

"Anything" I replied. I haven't been to the cinema for about thirty years, I think the last film I saw was ET.

At 2pm she picked me up and off we went to the cinema.

Well how it has changed, the amount of food people take in with them was the first thing I noticed.

Who can possibly eat a bucket of popcorn and drink a gallon of fizzy lemonade?

The last time I went all you had was a small Kiora orange squash and a two-ounce bag of liquorice comfits. It was enough!

I asked Emily what film she had chosen for us to watch?

"It's a sequel to Gone with the Wind, it's called Returned with the Gaviscon" said Emily

"Well I hope it's not a long as Gone with the Wind" I replied.

In my defence I didn't really take in what Emily had said.

We are watching a love story or as they call them now a RomCom. It's called Joan Bridges Diary or something.

The film was ok, it would have been better if it had had subtitles as I couldn't hear it above the munching and slurping sounds that surrounded me.

We also had a running commentary of what happens next from the women behind us who had obviously seen the film before.

Then her friend arrived late, with a wet raincoat draped over her arm, she then trailed her raincoat over everybody's heads in our row as she made her way to her seat behind us. My hair was ruined and she nearly knocked my Jelly Babies out of my hand with her wet coat.

"What have I missed? "she said to the women behind as she finally sat down.

We then had to listen to a commentary of what had happened in the film so far.

To add to the cinema experience the women in front of me had a beehive, I haven't seen that hairstyle for years.

This meant half the screen was blocked out. I spent two hours shuffling from side to side in order to see the film.

The other disappointment was there was no interval in which to get a choc ice.

I think it will be another thirty years before I go again.

Tuesday 21st April

Still Raining.

Some good news this morning Mrs Catterack phoned to say she had received a letter from the Highways Agency. They intend to investigate the electricity supplying to the traffic lights outside her house.

That's a good start.

Mrs Catterack has also gone to see a solicitor about compensation for all the years she has been over charged on her electricity bill.

She said "I have contacted Snograss, Snograss and Snograss solicitors in Snobihill. Unfortunately, Mr Snograss couldn't take up the case and neither could

Mr Snograss, so I have had to go with Mr Snograss! But I am sure he is as good as Mr Snograss and Mr Snograss." Mrs Catterack explained.

"I am sure he will be" I replied. I think that was the right answer!

No sooner had I put the phone down it rang again.

It was Jane Roid "Where are you?" She asked

"At home, otherwise I wouldn't have answered my home phone!" I said sarcastically

"I thought you were coming to this First aid course, set up by the U3A" said Jane

"I am when is it?" I enquired

"Now! We are about to start" said Jane

I dashed down to the Village Hall, I am getting very forgetful. I was sure it was next week but time seems to fly by these days.

When I arrived there were about ten people standing waiting for it to start. I stood next to the Major who was also attending.

The man at the front was dressed in his St Johns Ambulance uniform, so I assumed he was our tutor.

"Morning all, my name is Arthur Crown and I will lead you all through a basic first aid course. Now you will need a "Buddy" for this course, so please turn to the person next to you and introduce yourself if you do not know each other already" said Arthur

I looked desperately to my left but that person had already found his partner. Just at that moment my worst fears were realised when the Major tapped me on my back.

"I'm the Major very pleased to meet you" said the Major laughing.

This was a nightmare, especially when Arthur announced that our first activity would be "mouth to mouth" resuscitation.

I looked at the Major who was already chapsticking his lips in anticipation.

Thankfully Arthur produced a dummy patient for us to work with. This was laid on the floor.

Arthur then informed us about the do and don'ts when resuscitating someone.

He then acted out the procedure.

"Fred, Fred, are you ok?" He shouted at the dummy while shaking it.

"If Fred doesn't respond he is either dead, unconscious, or his name isn't Fred!" said Arthur.

Mrs Beaverbrook then asked "What do we do if it's not Fred?"

This was going to be a long morning!

That went ok as we all took turns to push Fred's chest to the rhythm of "Staying Alive".

Mrs Beaverbrook again missed the point and asked if she could sing another Bee Gees hit "Massachusetts" because it was her favourite.

Next we were shown how to stop a bleeding nose and finally how to put a sling on someone's arm.

I preceded to wrap the Major's arm in a sling but unfortunately the bandage I was using dropped to the floor and I got tangled around my feet.

To stop myself from falling over I grabbed hold of the Majors trouser braces which stretched about a yard but did thankfully prevent me from hitting the ground.

Unfortunately this made Majors trousers rise up his waist about twelve inches, upon which the Major let out a yelp, the sound he made reminded me of the time I accidently trod on Emily's dog's tail.

He fell to the floor obviously in a lot of pain. Arthur immediately came to his aid.

"My pants have gone so far up my arse, I think Ophelia has lacerated my haemorrhoids" he whispered to Arthur.

"Would you take a look?

Arthur then asked if we would all mind going into the side room while he had a look at the Majors backside.

As I stood by the door, I overheard Arthur's conversation with the Major "Well it's not a pretty sight" said Arthur

Too right, I thought, I had to paint it!

Arthur continued giving his diagnosis to the Major "The last time I saw anything like it, was when my daughter had a temper tantrum and stamped on a bunch of grapes in Tesco. I think I should call for an ambulance as I don't think you should sit down without an anaesthetic."

The ambulance arrived half an hour later and took the Major off to hospital on a stretcher, face down with his backside in the air.

I felt so bad but it was an accident.

Not the day I was expecting and certainly not the day the Major was expecting.

Wednesday 22nd April

Sunny at last

I felt so guilty this morning and didn't sleep well last night. I can't believe I put the Major in hospital.

Jane Roid phoned this morning and informed me that the Major had been kept in overnight.

I have no idea how she found out, she said she would visit him today and asked if I wanted to go with her.

I said yes but I am not so sure the Major will be very pleased to see me.

We arrived at the Hurtglands Hospital again, my fourth visit this year.

We checked with the receptionist as we arrived to see which ward the Major was on.

He is on the Anal Trauma Ward that's Ward 31" stated the Reception.

After what felt like a two mile walk and endless stairs, we arrived at the Ward 31.

There in bed at the end of the ward was the Major. He saw the two of us walking towards him.

"Watch out everyone, here's the "Lacerator" I told you all about, it looks like she severed someone else's piles on the way" Shouted the Major this caused me some embarrassment.

I suppose the black grapes I had in my hand was not the best thing to buy the Major.

The visit wasn't so bad in the end, the Major explained that the prostate examination had irritated his piles and at least now the Hospital have got them sorted.

It was a bit too much information to be honest, thankfully the Major should be home tomorrow.

"I must just say Ophelia, if ever I choke on anything and you're the only one around, just let me die!" stated the Major.

Jane dropped me back home after the visit.

Tomorrow is Pat Lardys funeral, I can't say I am looking forward to it. That was a stupid thing to write down whoever said "It's a funeral tomorrow and am I looking forward to it!"

I have heard that Pat's family have requested that people wear pink Pats favourite colour. This time though I am certainly wearing black, I don't care what anyone else is wearing I am not going through that embarrassment again after Stuarts funeral.

Thursday 23rd April

Raining well it would be it's funeral day.

Pats funeral is at 11am, so I spent the morning getting ready.

The funeral is at Burntwood Crematorium so Emily said she would take me as it is quite a drive.

She arrived dressed head to toe in pink!

There were so many mourners there when we arrived, everyone was in Pink. Great! Did I feel conspicuous!

The hearse then arrived with a very strange looking coffin in the back.

It looked like a slice of Victoria Sponge. Large at one end and going to a point at the other and painted to look like a slice of cake.

We did however get a clue to Pats weight, the eight bearers who carried the coffin in were sweating profusely under the weight of the coffin. I have never seen eight men so relieved to off load a casket.

Pat's sister Leana Lardy read the eulogy, it was explained that Pat had a fear of being certified dead when in fact she may still be alive. She had insisted that she have her mobile phone in the coffin just in case she wakes up.

Leana also said how passionate she was about her slimming Clubs and particularly the cake diet, her life time love of all things pink, whether it be her car, hair, clothes or the front door of her house.

It was just at that moment the phone in the coffin starting ringing, everyone went quiet and waited with bated breath. Would she answer it?

Then to everyone's horror Pat's voice boomed out from the casket, there were gasps and screams around the crematorium, three mourners fainted.

"Hello Pat here, I'm sorry I am eating cake at the moment and can't take your call. Please leave a message after the bleep".

Then someone else's voice boomed out from the coffin.

"Hi Pat, its Pedro. Will you please pick this up.......and stop being so elusive, I want that six grand you owe me for the tummy tuck operation and your sisters course of botox, your cheques bounced and I want my money. I will phone again later. Ciao".

Leana was led back to her pew in tears, she sat down sobbing and had to be consoled by her family.

We then all left to the sound of Scaffolds Lilly the Pink, Pat's favourite apparently.

Well after the shock of it all you can imagine what the topic of conversation was about at the wake. Talk about embarrassing.

I must say though credit to Pat's family, the vol au vents at the wake were the best I have ever tasted.

Home late afternoon, very tired after all that food.

Friday 24th April

Sunny day

Up all night! Not sure if it is because I am so nervous about the play tonight or those vol au vents.

I am also sweating profusely.

The morning didn't start well when I opened a brand-new roll on anti-perspirant and found it had already been used, it had a grey hair on the roll-on ball! This made me feel a little queasy but I had to use it as it was all I had.

Gail came around this morning to make me look presentable for my debut performance in "Back Side Story"

She arrived at 10.04 two minutes late!

No sooner had she burst through the door she was off. "Ar Wayne's bin on the throne all night, his arse looks like a red bottomed baboon its bin wiped that much, it's that Zal lav paper I told im not to buy it."

It was too much information really, but Gail thinks its nerves as Wayne can normally eat anything and not be ill.

"It ain elping him having to sing "Diarrhoea, I just ad a bout of diarrhoea" in the play itself" exclaimed Gail.

Gail titivated with my hair and painted my nails "Parkhurst Pink!".

All I did all day was pace up and down, I couldn't settle to do anything, I tried speeding up my Flossing routine in the mirror, but that just made matters worse as I looked like a three-year-old throwing a temper tantrum.

Emily arrived this afternoon, she was no better. "Look what I have done!" she said holding up her plastic Truncheon.

The truncheon had taken on the shape of a banana.

"I stupidly left it on the window sill and the sun must have bent it" she said almost in tears.

"It's a farce, it will be all the funnier for it being bent!" I said trying to console her.

Eventually the time came for us to go down to the Village Hall.

We arrived as instructed one hour before the performance was due to start.

Everard met us in the room at the back of the main hall. He was wearing a yellow string vest, black leather trousers and black Doc Martin boots.

"Attention Thespians I have some news" Everard cried out to a very crowded room.

"Dave and I have some very big news to reveal to you" he continued.

"Tonight's score will be played by the Kazoo Ensemble accompanied by the Swanee Whistle Quartet. So the music will be live!" he excitedly exclaimed.

"So that's what we can ere, I thought the Clangers ad bought in an infestation of bees" shouted Wayne.

Finally it was time for the curtain to go up, our adrenalin was up to max and we were off.

All those weeks of hard work for this two-hour play.

Emily loved the adulation, her bent truncheon and her Charlie Chaplin walk just caused raucous laughter which pleased Everard no end.

My flossing was hideous but it didn't matter, the more I messed up the more the audience loved it.

Wayne was exceptional and had everyone laughing, but still managed to get the audience and Everard crying when he died in Cordelia's arms in the closing scene after being stabbed with a wooden chip shop fork.

I think the fact that the play related to the working and upper classes went over everyone's heads, but no matter it was a good night and I loved every minute.

Saturday 25th April

Sunny again

Very upbeat this morning, I am still on a high from last night's performance.

I went down to the Two Stop shop this morning.

The Major was there talking to Angus Khan when I walked in.

"Here she is our very own Meryl Streep!" shouted the Major.

"I hope it is as good tonight, as I am going. I have a front row seat" said the Major.

"Perhaps we should get Ophelia to put her hand print on the payment for the Little Hampton, Hall of Fame" said Mr Khan.

For once I thought they were being serious but alas no.

When I got home the self-doubt set in again, even though everything went well last night.

I kept telling myself that even if it does go wrong it doesn't matter, but still the nerves started again.

The afternoon was spent practicing flossing, going over the few lines I had, and singing "I love the smell of formica"

Once again as if it was Groundhog day, Emily arrived and we walked down to the Village Hall at 6.30pm.

But sadly, today was very different from yesterday.

Everard and DRT greeted us dressed in top hat and tails, I have known idea why.

Everything was going to plan until I had to sing America now called formica. I corpsed and forgot the words. Everard had to prompt me from the wings. I was so embarrassed.

Then in the second half the dry ice machine went into overdrive, there was so much fog that the Kazoo Ensemble, Swannee Whistle Quartet and first six rows of the audience disappeared.

There was a lot of coughing and wheezy kazoo playing along with strange whistling sounds as they couldn't see their music sheets.

DRT shouted for us to just carry on regardless, so Wayne continued singing, "Tonight, tonight, I'll see my love tonight".

The Major who was on the front row of the audience shouted "Not in this bloody fog you won't!"

The dry ice machine was then kicked to face away from the stage and thankfully the fog soon dispersed.

But that wasn't the end of it, it now faced the door of the ladies toilet and very soon we heard a loud scream from inside the toilet, Mrs Catterack came bursting out in a panic. She thought the place was on fire.

I and everyone must have noticed that she was showing next weeks washing, her skirt was tucked into the top of her bloomers, thankfully Jane Roid informed her of her situation. Poor Mrs Catterack was so embarrassed.

The final scene was dramatic too, the wooden chip fork actually did get through Wayne's Donkey Jacket and really stabbed him. Wayne confirmed this by shouting "Yow stabbed me Ya Nutter"

We knew this wasn't in the script but fortunately the audience didn't and went into hysterical laughter.

DRT then bought the curtain down.

The audience just applauded thinking that was the end.

Wayne was whisked away to Hurtglands Hospital A & E. I would imagine he will be the only one at the hospital tonight stabbed by a chip fork!

I hope he is ok though.

Everard congratulated us all on our hard work and said he would reveal his next big production on Monday.

Not sure if I can stand the highs and lows of another play.

Sunday 26th April

Sunny and warm, Spring is in the air.

I went to Church this morning as it is a lovely day.

Father Aweigh greeted me at the gate "Congratulations Ophelia, I thoroughly enjoyed Friday night" said Father Aweigh

I just thanked him and carried on into Church. I then walked straight into the Major.

"I say old Gal that ending was quite traumatic last night, blood and everything. Great acting" said the Major.

Obviously for once he wasn't the first to know what had actually happened. I didn't say anything.

Then my phone rang, it was Everard "Hi Oprah!, just to let you know Wayne is ok, he had two large wooden splinters removed from his chest but he is fine, see you Monday. Ciao" and he rang off. I don't think I actually spoke.

I sat down reflecting on last night and how funny it had all been, I would miss it if I didn't go, so I will go on Monday.

During todays service two of our parishioners or should I say probably our eldest parishioners, Scott and Dotty Motty are re-taking their wedding vows to celebrate their platinum wedding anniversary.

This was so nice as they are a lovely couple always laughing and holding hands, you would thing they had just met.

I miss that so much.

Father Aweigh called them both to the front and asked Scott if he would take Dotty to be his wife. Scott replied with a smile "Do I have too, isn't seventy years enough?" then Scott and Dotty both got the giggles.

Scott then said "The day I don't hold her hand will be my last, the day I don't see her beautiful face will be the day I die. Of course, I will take her for my wife, never have I had an easier question to answer. I do"

Well there wasn't a dry eye in the Church, after the vows both Scott and Dotty knelt down at the alter to take communion, Scott had written on the soles of his shoes "Not" on the left and "Again" on the right which started everyone laughing again.

We then gave them a round of applause as they returned to their seats.

It was really lovely and made me think that so much is missing in my life, thankfully though I have some wonderful friends.

With so much going on I am not sure if I could find the time for a partner, but if it happens it happens.

I washed my sheets this afternoon, I could certainly do with a man to help me fold them and hang them up. That is always a struggle on your own.

Monday 27th April

Dry but blustery.

Not much point spending time on my hair this morning as I have to walk down to the drama class later and will get blown apart in this wind.

Emily arrived this afternoon with numerous ideas on how to fill the vacant slot left by the slimming club being closed.

She said she had found a Karate Club in Snobihill for the elderly, it is all done while sitting down!

That's useful if attacked I thought, providing you can find a chair to sit on!

Emily could see the puzzlement on my face.

"Well Connie Wobbles, you know Connie Wobbles who used to work at C & A. She's goes to it and Connie has progressed to a brown belt" Stated Emily shrugging her shoulders and looking at me as if I was mad!

Later we went down to the drama group, I am not quite sure what we will be doing now that "Back Side Story" has been performed.

Everard met us at the door, today he was wearing a postman's uniform?

"Have you got a new job?" I asked

"No, No, No. All will be revealed shortly" said Everard

It's always the big reveal with Everard, he loves it.

Once inside Everard rushed past us a leapt onto the stage where DRT was standing waiting.

"Friends, actors, thespians, lend me your ears" shouted Everard

We all faced him.

"You are probably wondering what do we do now and why am I dressed as a postman? Well I am about to tell you about our next production, it's another Farce as the last one was such a success" said Everard

He continued "I have had three scripts sent to me, one about a Slimming Club set in the wild west called "The Good, the Sad and the Cuddly" but as we have just lost Pat Lardy that didn't feel right.

Another I was keen on was set in the war called "Dad's Barmy!" but I have been told the word barmy can't be used any more such is the way of the world, so I left that well alone.

I have therefore gone for "Postman Pat always rings twice!" It looks such a funny script. There is a very raunchy scene between Pat and Mrs Goggin's across the post office counter in the second half, I shall have to reign that scene in. But apart from that it's fine.

I shall hand the scripts out for you to read over the next two weeks, as I am away on my "hols" in Benidorm next week. So no drama group next week." Said Everard.

DRT then spoke. "Can I just say what a privilege it has been working with you all, I have been offered a summer season at the end of Bournemouth Pier choreographing Scooby Doo on Ice!

Hopefully I will be back in October to choreograph your Panto. Thankyou!"

We all applauded DRT, Everard was in tears.

Well that was a day I didn't expect, I am worried now in case I get cast as Mrs Goggin's!

Tuesday 28th April

Raining

I was awoken at 8am by the phone ringing, it was Emily again.

"I just found something else to do tomorrow, over sixties chair dancing with some women called Iris" said Emily.

I was still half asleep so I said I would go. I have no idea what dancing with a chair can be though.

"Great" said Emily "It's 1pm tomorrow in Snobihill, I will pick you up at 12.20pm"

On that she put the phone down.

It was just as well I am up, as I am going to St Drongo's Primary School to talk to the children this morning.

I was told that all I have to do is chat with them about the past and my childhood.

How hard can it be?

I arrived at the school with a few other pensioners and was led by Mrs Butterscotch the Head into the main hall to await the children's arrival.

Twenty or so 6-year olds arrived in single file all holding clipboards and pens, four sitting to each Pensioner. My four introduced themselves as Albert, Cedric, Daisy and Empress!

They all when into fits of giggles when I told them my surname was Ramsbottom!

Wasting no time Cedric got straight to the point "How old are you?"

"Over seventy" I replied

"Did you know Queen Victoria?" asked Albert

"No, but did you know your name is the same as Queen Victoria's husband" before I had chance to finish another question came my way from Empress.

"Is your hair made from silver?" asked Empress

"No, it's just grey" I replied

"Why?" asked Albert

I didn't know what to say really.

"Did you know, when I was a child there were no mobile phones, no computers and hardly anyone had a car?" I stated trying to get back on track.

"Yes" said a very precocious Cedric

"Can you take your teeth out? My Grandma can!" asked Empress

"No" I replied.

I was then subjected to a barrage of questions, I hardly had chance to finish answering one before another was asked. My brain was frazzled by the end.

I then realised Daisy hadn't spoken.

"What do you want to do when you grow up?" I asked her

"A Nurse like Mummy used to be!" said Daisy

"Used to be?" I enquired

"Daddy said Mummy is looking after the Angels now" replied Daisy

I didn't know what to say, I wanted to hug her but that's not allowed anymore. "I am sure she is Daisy and aren't those angels lucky Mummy's there" I said trying to compose myself.

Thankfully soon afterwards it finished and Mrs Butterscotch thanked us as did the children.

Afterwards I sat in the car in school car park and cried for a good ten minutes.

I then reflected on how lucky I have been in my life!

Wednesday 29th April

Sunny Intervals

A quiet morning watching TV and the world of celebrities. How did we become so obsessed with other people's lives?

We had some "Breaking News" while I was watching. Elton John's aunt will have her bunions sorted today afterall, thanks to Elton's intervention.

I do hope she will be ok!   Like I care. What drivel, I turned it off as I was getting annoyed.

Emily arrived at 12 O'clock.

I have always wondered why we say O clock what does the O stand for!?

We arrived in Snobihill in good time for the Chair Dancing! I was intrigued.

The dancing was at 2pm not 1pm as Emily thought, 1pm was the Karate class.

So we went and had a coffee at the Coff and Drop café.

On returning for the dancing class the karate class were just leaving their class, we waited while all these elderly people dressed in their white martial arts outfits filed out of the room.

It was like a Bruce Lee appreciation society reunion. But if it keeps them fit why not.

We then went into the room which now had a smell of stale sweat and winter green ointment.

A lady stood at the front dressed in a black leotard.

"Hello" said Emily "You must be Iris, we spoke on the phone?"

"No, I'm Clodagh, are you Emily?" she replied in a strong Irish accent. "Yes "replied Emily

"Well if you and your friend would like to take a seat my son Declan will be here shortly and all you have to do if follow his lead. If you can stand all well and good but most of our Members do the dancing sitting down" said Clodagh

Emily and I turned around and there if front of us was about twenty pensioners all dressed in black leotards. We felt very conspicuous both dressed in pink.

The seats were arranged in a single row in an arc facing Clodagh with a large space between us. We sat on the only two seats available in the middle.

Then the music started, I think it was from Riverdance.

Then it dawned on me, I turned to Emily "It's Irish dancing, what have you got us into now?" I was so annoyed.

"Remember to keep your arms down straight by your sides" shouted Clodagh

At this point Declan ran into the middle of the floor in front of us leaping in the air like a gazelle on heat.

His legs going ten to the dozen as he performed his Irish dance routine.

Two ladies stood up but the rest remained seated with their legs trying to emulate Declan's.

Emily and I stayed in our chairs. We did feel ridiculous Irish dancing while seated.

Ten minutes in we were exhausted.

By the time we had we had finished I could hardly walk, my knees were in tatters.

I was tempted to take one of the Zimmer frames by the door to help me get back to the car park.

I don't think I be rushing out to get a black leotard anytime soon.

Emily was much the same.

We held each other for support and had another cup of coffee before going home.

Thursday 30th April

Lovely day, Sunny

The sun shone through my bedroom window this morning, a lovely day until I tried to step out of bed.

My legs are still really painful.

It is my own fault whatever made me think I could keep up with Declan yesterday.

Even though I was sitting down my legs were still going like the clappers for a whole hour.

I did enjoy it though as daft as it looked and felt. I am sure it will get easier.

I didn't get up until about ten o'clock.

I had to get up, as I had run out of bread, so I very slowly ventured down to the Two Stop Shop.

To give you some idea how slow I was walking such was the pain, Wendy Miller and Oscar her guide dog caught me up!

He seemed much better, although Oscar was wearing bright yellow earmuffs and what looked like swimming goggles?

Wendy informed me that Oscar's hearing was much better since the cochlear implants had been fitted but he finds the traffic very loud, so he wears the earmuffs when out.

"The goggles?" I enquired

"The optician did try him with contact lenses, but he didn't like me putting them in. So the Optician recommended prescription swimming goggles." explained Wendy

I have no idea how that works, do dogs have an eye test!

 I Imagined the optician saying to Oscar "Bark once if that's clearer" when doing the test.

I entered the shop and Mr Khan shouted, here she is Little Hampton's very own answer to Michael Flatley.

Will you give us a jig before you go?

"Just a loaf please" I replied and walked out.

How do people in this Village get to know everything instantly?

I can't believe that we are 120 days into the year, if ever the rest of the year is a manic as the first 120 days, I think I will go mad.

Two Funerals, four Hospital visits, endless mis-haps and fighting for justice on so many fronts.

Looking back though there have been so many funny moments too.

Even if they did not seem funny at the time. Nearly being held in a care home, so many moments at the Drama Class, almost being paired off with a Russian on a Blind date and not forgetting the Major posing at the art class, if only I could forget it!

I sat down in my chair at home and giggled to myself.

Yes, there have been sad moments, but being in the autumn of your life in isn't so bad really!

Actually, I am probably in the winter of my Life, perish the thought!

Printed in Great Britain
by Amazon